Confessions of Love

UNO CHIYO

· ·

Confessions of Love

TRANSLATED BY PHYLLIS BIRNBAUM

University of Hawaii Press

Honolulu

Originally published as *Iro Zange*
© Uno Chiyo 1935

English translation published by
University of Hawaii Press
© 1989 Phyllis Birnbaum

95 94 93 92 91 89   6 5 4 3 2

Portions of *Confessions of Love*
have appeared in an altered
form in *The New Yorker,*
Translation, and *Crosscurrents*

Library of Congress Cataloging-in-Publication Data

Uno, Chiyo, 1897–
  [Iro zange. English]
  Confessions of love / Uno Chiyo ; translated by Phyllis Birnbaum.
    p.   cm.
  Translation of: Iro zange.
  ISBN 0–8248–1170–4 — ISBN 0–8248–1176–3 (pbk.)
    1. Tōgō, Seiji, 1897–1978—Fiction.   I. Title.
PL840.N58I7613 1989   88–39612
895.6'34—dc19   CIP

TRANSLATOR'S NOTE

Uno Chiyo (1897–) is one of Japan's most eminent writers. She is known for an elegant writing style which has been admired since the beginning of her professional career in the 1920s. Uno was also famous for her beauty, and her private life—tumultuous by the standards of any period—has found its way into much of her fiction.

Uno Chiyo was born in Iwakuni in southwestern Japan, but by her own accounts she was altogether unsuited for life in the conservative Japanese provinces. Uno seems to have been precocious not only in her literary interests, but also in her talent for choosing just the behavior that would most outrage the local citizenry. Her mother died when she was still an infant, and after her father remarried there were five more children in the family. Although Uno's stepmother treated them well, her father was harsh, imposing many restrictions upon the household. Uno recalls that the children both feared and loved him, but there is little evidence of his attractive side in her reminiscences. "My father's prohibitions became the law in our house and we did not find this unreasonable," Uno writes in one of her autobiographical stories. "The snow would fall. I didn't wear anything on my feet on my way to school and walked across the snow barefoot. . . . In order to avoid people's pitying remarks, I would take the back roads and never felt that my feet were cold."

After her father's death in 1913, Uno, the oldest child, was left to fend for her family. Then, as in later years, she demonstrated dazzling pluck as well as a genius for emotional catastrophe. Uno's appearance caused problems from the start, since she could not bring herself to blend quietly into the general population. In the opinion of the head of the primary school where she eventually taught, Uno dressed in kimonos that were too flashy for a schoolteacher. Moreover, Uno became convinced that her dark complexion was magically, beautifully transformed by face powder and would not go anywhere without her makeup. When she arrived at the school wearing her makeup for the first time, her lovely glow caused a sensation among the teachers and students. She received a love letter written in blood, then a marriage proposal that ended in a sexual assault; she finally lost her teaching job when she became involved in a forbidden romance with another teacher. She went to Korea to escape from this scandal, but once she realized that the teacher she had left behind wanted nothing more to do with her, she rushed back home from Seoul to confront him. Coincidentally, she had purchased a knife on her way over to his house and his discovery of the weapon hidden in her kimono added considerably to the complexity of the moment.

In 1917 Uno went to Tokyo, where she worked very briefly as a waitress. Fortunately the restaurant was close to Chūō Kōron Sha, the noted publishing house, and many well-known writers and editors came to eat there. She did not forget those early literary acquaintances even after she left Tokyo to marry her cousin and live in the north. In Sapporo, "the winter came early. . . . The snow reached the house's eaves and throughout the day I could hear the sleigh bells." Although Uno says that she was content simply to stay at home waiting for her husband's return, domestic tranquility was never to be her forte. It is difficult to believe that she had only the Hokkaidō snowflakes on her mind during the many restless hours she spent watching the blizzards blow outside her window.

Eventually Uno took up sewing to earn some money and soon purchased a new home for herself and her flabbergasted husband. This modest Sapporo residence, which lacked all basic necessities, was the first of more than a dozen residences Uno would acquire over the coming decades. "I always build a house when I start something new in my life," she has written. "I'm like a snail crawling along with a shell on its back. I first build a house and then I start roaming around. Maybe I feel that I'll stabilize the insecure life I'm about to begin."

While Uno was still in Sapporo, she came upon a Tokyo newspaper which asked readers to submit short stories for a contest. Uno sent a story—"The Powdered Face"—and true to literary miracle, it won the first prize. Exhilarated by this success and astonished at the money a single short story could bring, Uno promptly set out to write another work. She sent this to no less a personage than the esteemed editor of Chūō Kōron Sha whom she knew from her waitressing days. When she received no reply about the fate of her manuscript, Uno resolutely went to Tokyo herself, in the spring of 1922, to find out if anyone had even read it. She planned to return to her husband in a few days, and left a mountain of dirty clothes and dishes to be attended to upon her return. Once she reached Tokyo, she immediately went to see the editor. He was apparently irritated by her questions and answered by showing her the latest issue of *Chūō Kōron* magazine, where her story had just been published.

In the excitement of this success, Uno forgot the charm of Sapporo's sleigh bells and the husband she had left behind. She had come to Tokyo with the intention of staying only long enough to find out about her manuscript, but once there she gave up her former existence and started afresh with gusto. She had in fact met her next husband, Ozaki Shirō, in the course of this short visit. Then, as in other times in her life, Uno proved capable of dropping everything—literally leaving the dirty dishes in the sink—to run off to a new book, a new house, a new man. Her writings gain much of their verve from the excitement, and the desperation, of those experiences.

Uno went on to establish herself as a writer who specialized in chronicling the stormy vicissitudes of love. Many of her writings are based upon her own romantic adventures, and her best-known works, *Confessions of Love* (*Iro Zange*, 1935), "The Puppet Maker Tenguya Kyūkichi" (*Ningyōshi Tenguya Kyūkichi*, 1942), *Ohan* (1957; trans., 1961), and "To Sting" (*Sasu*, 1966; trans., 1982), won her a devoted readership. Uno's intense tales of love lost, revived, then lost again can become mere romantic fluff, but at her best she captures a very human craziness as her Japanese lovers try to settle matters between them once and for all. Her prose style has also brought her much praise: "rich, supple, sensual," according to one Japanese critic, "overflowing with womanly feelings." She also has a gift for quirky characterizations, and her male characters—more often than not utterly despicable—are memorable. The woman who keeps reappearing in Uno's writings loves unwisely, gaining our sympathy with the immensity of her affections. This fervent woman throws herself at one undeserving man after another, but she has sufficient canniness and resilience to pick herself up after the tempests have passed.

In addition to her reputation as a writer, Uno is also known for her interest in fashion. At one time, with the help of another husband, the writer Kitahara Takeo, she published *Style (Sutairu)*, a popular women's magazine. Now a grande dame of Japanese letters, Uno has in the past few years become the subject of much media attention in Japan. In fact, there has been an "Uno Chiyo Boom." Her life story was serialized on television and movies made from her books. She continues to be active in her literary pursuits. Uno has received the Noma Prize and many other literary awards.

Confessions of Love is based upon the sensational romantic career of the artist Tōgō Seiji. Uno says that she got the idea for this novel when she was writing *Why Are the Poppies Crimson? (Keshi wa naze kurenai,* 1930) and had decided to include a love suicide scene involving gas inhalation. She felt that she could not quite convey the emotional pressures of the moment without further research and so she telephoned Tōgō, who had just emerged alive from a highly publicized love suicide attempt. She asked him if he would please give her some insight into the man's side of the entire experience. Tōgō delicately saw that such things should not be described over the telephone and agreed to meet her at a bar where they could discuss the matter in person. He arrived there in the very best of post–suicide pact chic, with his recently slashed neck covered by a white bandage.

Tōgō did not immediately recount his story, but invited Uno back to his home where they spent the night together on the same blood-stained futon that had been used for the failed double suicide. The invitation to sleep on that very futon won over Uno's reckless heart and although she had come with only her handbag as luggage, once again intending only a brief visit, she remained with Tōgō for five years.

Initially the liaison was extremely happy, since she and Tōgō had both been through enormous personal upheavals and relished the peace of their life together. The strains began to show, however, after they started to build a splendid house that was rather beyond their means. It was to be a completely Western-style residence, somewhat in the manner of Le Corbusier, with atelier, salon, and fancy bedroom. But they could not meet the expenses on their gorgeous home and were frequently harassed by creditors. Uno was forced to travel around selling Tōgō's paintings for the cash they so desperately required. She had no time for her own writing and Tōgō rightfully suspected that she had become romantically involved with some of her customers.

It was only after they had almost finished paying for the house—a quiet period she likens to the aftermath of a lengthy war—that Uno began to record Tōgō's reminiscences. The tale of his great romance, which took him a year to relate, eventually became *Confessions of Love*. Uno claims that she didn't change a single word of Tōgō's narration and wrote down exactly what he said, only urging him on occasionally by asking what happened next. She gives full credit for the book's success to Tōgō's skillful way of telling his own story.

This novel is often seen as a chronicle of the 1920s, when the so-called "modern girls" flourished in Japan. These progressive women were known not only for their bobbed hair, but also for their attempts to challenge old and repressive attitudes about a woman's place in society. Undeniably, *Confessions of Love* shows three independent, "modern" women experimenting with new freedoms, but by contemporary standards their behavior hardly raises an eyebrow. Reading the novel today, one is more likely to be struck by the extraordinary nature of the male narrator.

Although Uno says that she has merely recorded Tōgō's version of events word-for-word, there is the conviction throughout that he would have surely fashioned a more attractive picture of himself in these pages had he been the author of his own reminiscences. As Uno slyly presents him, the narrator (named Yuasa Jōji in the novel) has a way with women, but his allures are mixed with a terrible passivity. He whips his romances up to a crescendo but can go no further, and so he shatters his own life as well as the lives of his lovers. Weak men who are irresistible to women are a specialty of Japanese literature and while Western readers may fail to fathom Yuasa's charms, to a Japanese audience he is a familiar romantic hero. One cannot help suspecting that Uno, a woman author given free reign over a man's confessions, took delight in arranging the story so as to emphasize the darkest sides of her narrator's character. At times it seems clear that Uno has left Tōgō's words behind to write a not-so-subtle condemnation of his behavior. She herself probably could not help feeling that she had wasted years of her life in thrall to such men. Uno is surely at her best when she conveys the folly and the inevitability of such attractions.

Uno recalls that *Confessions of Love* "took me about two years to complete. During that time the story was out of Tōgō Seiji's hands and became my complete responsibility. I even got the crazy idea that I myself was the creator of this work and I wrote feverishly." A modern reader cannot help feeling that Uno shaped Tōgō's tale with fury and pleasure—these emotions, may I say, have spurred on the translator also.

In this translation names follow Japanese order, with the family name first. I am grateful to the National Endowment for the Arts for the grant that enabled me to translate this novel. I am deeply indebted to Teruko Ugaya Craig and Stuart Kiang, my editor at the University of Hawaii Press, for their generous assistance.

Confessions of Love

"I wonder where I should start?" he said, reflecting for some time before slowly starting to speak:

I'd been living abroad and as soon as I returned home I rented a small house in Kamata with three rooms downstairs and two upstairs. Since I occupied the upstairs and my wife and child the downstairs, we led almost completely separate lives. We had decided to get a divorce some time before that and were only waiting for a few details to be settled. I must say that I found myself absolutely charmed by the beauty of the Japanese women I had not seen for ten years. As soon as I woke up I would rush out of the house to roam through the streets and prowl the dance halls and cafés. It would be very late before I returned home and I often didn't see my wife for days.

One night I came home to find a letter lying on my desk, written in a woman's handwriting. The signature read "Takao" and I assumed it had come from a woman whose family name was Takao, but when I opened the envelope I saw my mistake at once: the name inside was Komaki Takao. I suppose you could say it was appropriate that such vigorous handwriting would come from a woman with a man's name like Takao. After two pages of a poem that made no sense at all, she wrote that her home was near the Tokugawa estate in Sendagaya and why didn't I drop by for a visit. Actually, as far as love letters go, this one was rather abstract and simple. I read it casually and soon dropped off to sleep. But the next day I found the same sort of letter on my desk when I came home, and this time, after the poem, she requested a reply. The next day and the next, more of those same envelopes arrived. I didn't feel like opening them, so I just left them as they were. The barrage of letters continued for about a week until one day she switched from the long thin envelope she had been using to a large Western-style envelope. I didn't have anything particular in mind when I opened this one, but I found, tucked into the letter, a photograph of a young woman in a very serene and middle-class setting. Behind her was a chair draped with a tiger skin, and a piano. The next morning as I was going out, I showed the photo to my wife.

"Oh, it looks as if they're rich! You've been seeing her, haven't you?"

"Nonsense—do you really think I'd see some woman who keeps writing me letters?"

"But it wouldn't be so bad if you saw a little of her, now would it? She definitely has money."

My wife was trying to sound sophisticated when she spoke like this, but actually the woman in the photograph was only good-looking enough to treat as lightly as she was suggesting. After that the letters kept on coming. Of course I didn't think they had affected me at all, but I couldn't get over the woman's tenacity. I'd ask the women I met at the dance halls and cafés, "Do you happen to know someone named Komaki Takao?" So I suppose you could say she was much on my mind. One night I came home and picked out a letter from the small pile by my desk and opened it. There was no poem in this one, only three lines of writing:

> Tomorrow night from 6:00 to 6:30, I'll be waiting at the ticket gate at Sendagaya Station. Come and meet me. I'll be wearing an artificial red rose in my hair.

Since I obviously had not gone to meet her, I wondered about the next day's note and read the letter with the following day's postmark, only to discover that she had written the same thing word for word: ". . . I'll be wearing an artificial red rose in my hair." My curiosity piqued, I read the letter that was postmarked the day before the one I'd first opened and there was the same message about the artificial rose. The next one I opened and the next were identical. I ended up flabbergasted to find twelve or thirteen letters, including the one that had come that day, all with the same message. I decided to go back to the earlier letters and read the first two or three. The seven or eight before the letters about the rose contained the photo of the young woman and the tiger skin, and preceding those there was more of that nonsensical poem. As I sat there surrounded by a pile of her letters I had to admit I was beginning to feel the stirrings of a strange interest in this woman. I decided to try to see her.

The next night I got to Sendagaya Station after six twenty. I was halfway down the staircase to the platform when I saw, at the ticket gate, a tall young woman standing very straight, facing in my direction, with her long hair braided and twisted loosely on her head like the photographs of Madame Felicita that were then always in the magazines. She was wearing an artificial red rose. It was a summer evening and still light out, but the bright electric lights of Meiji Gaien Park directly behind made it difficult to see her face. I'm still not sure whether I imagined this but I felt she was younger and livelier than her photograph. As I approached she raised eyes sparkling with light and looked me square in the face. I made myself walk slowly past her and went left at the open space in front of the rickshaw stand, then along the path. I somehow felt her eyes following me, but at such times you can hardly walk up to someone and say, "Tell me, are you Komaki-san?" Once beyond her line of vision, I stopped to look back at the station through the trees. She had resumed her former position with her back to me, evidently unaware of who I was. I watched her until she turned around at precisely six thirty and left the station in the direction of the Tokugawa estate. She departed with the brisk precise movements of a machine, showing no signs of regret.

I waited a bit before I followed her. A block from the station she turned right beyond the Tokugawa estate on the corner and soon disappeared behind a stone gate even more impressive than theirs. The name on the gate was Komaki Yoshirō. The entrance to the garden was like a tunnel lined with old rose bushes, and I stood there, as if dumbstruck, straining my ears for the sound of her sandals, which I could still hear inside the garden. Soon after, when I asked the owner of a rice shop near Hachiman Shrine about the family, he told me that the house belonged to an important Mitsubishi official who was often away on trips to China and Taiwan. While he was abroad, his only daughter, who attended a school for girls from noble families, was left home alone. At that point, to be honest, it was the thrill of the chase that urged me on as I wondered if I had just followed the daughter of that house. But, actually, when I thought again of the woman I had seen for just an instant at the ticket gate—with her tall, stern figure and the glittering light in her eyes when she looked up at me—I couldn't imagine feeling anything romantic about her since she didn't seem to have the slightest trace of softness or sentimentality. Even so, as I was spending most of my time those days making the rounds of dance halls and cafés and seeing only the kind of women who frequented such places, this woman struck me as something fresh and different. I went directly home that night without looking for further entertainment. When I reached my house there was, just as I had anticipated, another letter with the line about the red rose on my desk.

The next day I left my house earlier than usual, stopped at the barber shop, and on the way had my shoes shined. When I reached the Sendagaya platform the woman was standing very straight, in the same pose as the previous day, but upon recognizing me she walked straight over with an air of conviction, obviously feeling no hesitation. "You're Yuasa-san, aren't you? It is Yuasa-san, isn't it?"

When I confirmed this, she said, "You came yesterday too, didn't you?" For some reason I felt like being evasive, so I said no, this was the first time I had come. "That's not true," she replied, "but since you left so quickly, I did think for a moment it was someone else."

"You've been waiting here every day?"

"Yes. You see, I knew you'd come one day." She started to walk on ahead. As I followed, I took note of her shapely hands and legs and the wholesome color in her cheeks.

"Why have you been writing me every day?"

"You really shouldn't ask that. If you hadn't come I would have kept on writing for three months or even three years. I'm not the type who gives up on something halfway, you know." She turned to me in front of the stone gate I had seen the previous day. "Won't you come in for a minute?"

I followed her through the tunnel of rose bushes and into a Western-style annex in the back garden. The rooms inside were already dark. When she turned the lamp on, the room was dimly lit but I could make out the chair with the tiger skin and the piano from the photographs, and also my photo, apparently from a newspaper clipping, pinned to the wall.

"Won't you have something to drink?" she said, offering me some Western liquor.

Close up, I saw that her expression was almost babyish and that she looked more like a child than a woman. That quality seemed to explain her lack of fear.

"Whatever gave you the idea that you wanted to meet me?"

"Why do you keep bringing that up?" She smiled slightly. "Because I like you. You see, I am in love with you."

"You're in love with me?" I had to laugh. "You say that, but tell me, have you ever been in love before?"

"Certainly. The first time was with my tutor, but once I saw how stupid it all was I fired him myself."

Time had passed but no one else had come into the annex. Nor had there been any sounds from the main house either.

"Tell me," I continued to press her, "exactly how did you decide that you liked me?"

"It started when I met you on the train."

Her story began with the day I had returned to Japan, when she and I happened to be on the same train from Kobe to Tokyo. She had gone to Osaka to meet her father, who was returning from Taiwan. They had been in the dining car and had just returned to their seats when I came in after them with the fan she had forgotten. "This is yours, isn't it?" I had said, handing it to her father. I did remember the incident, but that girl—she must have been this same one—had been wearing a navy blue school uniform and had been knitting, looking down the whole time. I couldn't recall her at all, other than as a semblance of the white-haired gentleman with the fleshy forehead and piercing gaze seated beside her. When the train reached Tokyo Station that evening, my family and friends were there and, seeing me surrounded by reporters and photographers, she had wondered who I could be. She eagerly checked the next day's newspaper and learned that I was the Western-style artist Yuasa Jōji, settled back home in Kamata after a long stay abroad. As long as her father was at home, however, she could do nothing about seeing me.

"You see, I'm very good at being two completely different people depending on the situation," she said. "When my father is at home I'm a very well behaved and proper young lady. When he goes away I become a troublemaker no one can control." If the situation required it, she went on, she could play the kind of perfectly refined daughter who has maidservants at each elbow and is not even permitted to look out the car window. Her other role as the delinquent girl she felt she did better.

She had hoped her father would go to Taiwan again soon but she had to wait twenty days before finally seeing him off at Tokyo Station, whereupon she turned around and went immediately to the Kamata police station to look up my address and some information about my family. She then went by my house in a rickshaw to have a look and even considered going in, but changed her mind at the last minute and returned home. After that she wrote letters to me every day.

"Then you know that I have a wife and child—"

"So?" She pouted. "That's your problem. It doesn't bother me. I don't know what kind of wife you have, but I'm sure you'll like me much better."

"Oh, and how can you tell?"

"I just know." She repeated this as if talking to herself and then looked up at me: "To think that a person like you . . . How can you paint, living in such a house?"

She fell silent and as I studied her profile I somehow grasped what she was trying to say. This coddled young lady, who attended a school for daughters of the nobility, apparently pitied me for my way of life. Or at the very least, she was concerned about my circumstances. I became sullen, as if a mere child had called me a fool. To hide my bad mood I quietly took hold of her hand.

"Not allowed. No touching permitted," she protested, moving off toward the corner of the room, where she riveted her eyes on me. I didn't pursue her and finally saying that it was getting late, I went out. She followed, to see me off at the train. "See you tomorrow," she said as we parted.

But the next day I didn't feel like going out. As someone I could love, this woman, with her direct manner and wholesome body, had failed to touch my heart. To be frank about it, I preferred women who were good-looking, and a woman like that, who was no great beauty, could hardly have inspired me to go seriously chasing after her.

The days passed and I became busy with the work I was going to show at a fall exhibition. "It's a sin to neglect a woman who burns for you like this . . . If you don't come to see me, I don't know what I'll do," she wrote in the letters that came, as usual, every day.

One night I decided to entertain for a change and invited friends like the singer Kamei Yūjirō and the painter Sonoda Shūkichi over to the second floor of my house. My wife was serving us and we were drinking beer when we heard a child's voice from below. My wife went down and soon called up to me from the staircase: "It's that woman. She says she wants to see you." She had evidently gone to the local vegetable store, where she had asked one of the children to come over and summon me. As my wife related this, the expression on her powdered white face hardened—even though she'd been the one who had coolly suggested that I go and amuse myself with the woman in the photograph.

Since I didn't feel like discussing it all over again, I shouted down to her. "Just ignore it. It's up to her if she wants to stand out there and wait."

"But she's got some nerve. Sending you all those weird letters. And now she has someone come over to call for you."

"What's the matter?" Kamei asked with an officious look on his face.

My wife, who had rejoined us, slumped down onto the floor and venomously told him about the woman. Kamei turned to me. "It isn't right to let this go on without doing anything. If you're not interested, then you've got to make it clear to her. She's got to hear it from your own lips that you're turning her down."

"But even if I turn her down, it'll be the same thing all over again."

Half an hour must have gone by when a man from the local rickshaw stand turned up at the front door to ask me to step out for a few minutes and meet her. I told him I'd come soon and sent him away, but then Kamei looked at me very seriously. "You can't just leave her waiting there. Your wife and the rest of us are sitting here, so now's the time to tell her what you think—here, in front of all of us." Kamei then went off to get the woman, more out of nosy curiosity, I suspected, than real concern. He soon came back with her, but by then our dinner had taken on the air of a solemn conference. My wife sat farthest away, staring at the woman with a look of sheer hostility.

"We were just talking about this matter," Kamei said to Takao. "Isn't it rather odd, a young woman like you getting so worked up about a man like Yuasa-kun?"

"And what do you mean by that?" She looked at Kamei as though cross-examining him.

"Well, what I mean is that you know Yuasa-kun is married and has a child."

"I know all about that, but it has nothing to do with me."

"What did she say?" my wife shouted, enraged.

"Please now, leave this to me," Kamei urged. "Listen, Komaki-san, what I'm saying may be only simple common sense, but you know there is no future in this."

"I don't know that at all."

At that point, I suppose the only thing she could do nothing about was her attraction to me. And from the way she had just spoken, she clearly didn't have a shred of respect for my wife. Kamei let out with a groan, then both he and my wife turned fidgety and impatient. Takao was the only calm person present. Finally Kamei told her, "I'll see you home. You needn't worry, nothing will happen." They left together, and from the second floor railing my wife watched Kamei's tall, thin figure disappear behind the neighbor's hedge. "Why am I surrounded by men who are such weaklings?" she exclaimed with considerable irritation in her voice.

The next day Kamei came by some time after noon. "You're a fool," he announced as soon as he walked in. "You know who Komaki Yoshirō is? He's the famous Komaki Yoshirō of Mitsubishi. And you're letting such good luck just slip away? That young lady's not bad, by the way—what do you think? How many women would come out and say just what they think so clearly?"

"Too clearly. She's crazy."

"But that kind of craziness can be interesting. You won't find too many women from the lower classes with a flavor like that." He lowered his voice a bit, explaining that on the way to her house the previous night he had promised he would take me there that day.

"There won't be any scene, so do me a favor and make good on my word."

"Oh, all right, stop nagging. I'll go for your sake." So before I really knew what I was saying, I had apparently accepted Kamei's offer to serve as a go-between.

After dusk we went to her house together. At the front entrance Kamei stepped out ahead to announce himself; then we waited for some time in a large, old-fashioned parlor until the door opened and in walked Komaki Takao, unsmiling as usual. "Kamei-san, your work is over now," she declared abruptly, not looking at me. The maid brought in some ice cream and Kamei took his in haste. "You don't mind if I stay here long enough to eat this, do you?" he said, apparently having decided to assume a clowning attitude with Takao. But as soon as he was finished he hastily departed, leaving me alone with her. Silent for a moment, she soon asked if we could go out. A trip to Ginza for tea was what I had in mind when I agreed and suggested that we leave, but just then the maid came in with tea and cake.

"Is that matter we discussed all settled?" she asked the maid.

"Yes, and the taxi has already come," the servant replied.

We went out the back door and found a big automobile waiting. It was only after seating myself beside her in the car that I decided to inquire, "Tell me, what about your Mama?" This was actually nothing to me, but according to Kamei, the mother was supposed to be in the house when the father was away.

"Mama has her own way of having a good time." Takao blinked as she said this, looking at me coldly. Later I found out that this arrogant, wayward woman had learned all she knew from her mother.

So that night, I, a man already thirty-two, was taken by an eighteen-year-old woman to a hotel—the same one her mother used for her trysts. In fact, it was the hotel arrangements that she had been asking the maid about. As we made our way through the dark streets, raindrops splashed against the window, soon becoming a driving storm. I tried to figure out where we were by studying the lights that flickered through the rain, but my vague recollections of the Tokyo streets I had known ten years before were immediately extinguished in the heavy downpour. I was at a loss to guess even our general direction, but still I didn't think to ask Takao or the driver where we were going. I would go wherever I was bound to go, and for that matter I found the deliberate way she sat in complete silence rather comical.

The car stopped and a man wearing a white uniform came running out from behind a dark stand of trees to offer us an umbrella. We had arrived at the hotel. I was under the impression that we might be having dinner there and I followed Takao as she quite calmly made her way through a lobby lined with politely nodding bellboys. We turned down a dark hall and one of the bellboys ran up from behind to hand her a key. She opened the door to one of the rooms and after I followed her in she locked it firmly.

"This is shocking," I said to her. "You're doing what the man is supposed to do. I'm supposed to be doing this for you."

"You're quite right." She stood by the locked door with a hostile glint in her eyes, breathing hard. "But today I'm going to do everything. I'm going to do what the man is supposed to do."

As I stood there too stupefied to move, she went over to the bed and began removing the light red kimono she was wearing. Once the obi was off, her whole kimono slipped down onto the bed and her naked body, without a stitch of clothing on, was astonishingly alluring. I would not have dreamed it possible from what she looked like when fully dressed, but the softness of her white skin made me feel that if I put my hand there it might stay attached forever, never letting go. She was probably only too aware that there was not a man alive who could remain unmoved by the sight of her naked body. I was in a daze as I fought to quiet my heart, which had suddenly blazed up like a wild animal just shown some food. Strangely enough, as an artist I had never felt until that moment such an instinctive desire to possess a woman's lovely flesh, but the sight of this woman's body overpowered me, annihilating other desires and all self-control. I suddenly found myself wondering about the love affair between this woman and her teacher.

"What are you daydreaming about? Are you that much of a coward?"

Her voice lashed like a whip against my cheek. I swallowed hard. What was she saying? When provoked like that, what does a man do? She must surely have known. In spite of myself, I took her in my arms roughly and threw her down on the bed. Shoulders heaving, she opened her eyes wide as if to challenge my next move. But I had gone wild and I buried my face between her soft breasts, moving my hands over her body. Even when she let out a small cry I didn't stop. If I had been able to speak I would have said, "Watch and you'll see what I'm going to do— By the time this night is over, your body won't exist anymore." Suddenly she writhed and pushed me up with both her hands. Then she went crazy, biting me all over my arms and chest. What could this mean? Before, she had taunted me, challenged me, and now she was resisting so fiercely? I let her go on but didn't release my hold. When she dropped her head back and closed her eyes, a thin line of blood dripped from her pale lips. I called to her, shaking her by her shoulders. By then I'd lost all sense of time. When I finally threw myself down on the bed exhausted, the white of dawn had begun to shine through the curtains and I fell into a deep sleep. It was close to noon by the time I woke. She was still sleeping as soundly as the dead, not stirring even though I tried to rouse her several times. When I got up and had a look around, I saw my torn white shirt and the fingernail marks on my cheeks and arms. Suddenly afraid she would awaken, I gathered my things and left the hotel. In the front garden the hydrangeas were blooming with a malign abundance under the blazing July sun. I was seized with such a severe dizziness that I thought I would collapse on the spot.

. . .

After that I found myself wondering about Komaki Takao from time to time, vaguely anticipating a letter summoning me, but one day passed, then another, and there was no word. It seemed odd that her letters should stop coming when she had been so regular about writing to me every day. On my way home late at night I would tell myself that today I'd receive a letter, but when I did get home I'd find nothing. After five or six days had passed, my wife came up to the second floor with a business card, saying that a man she didn't know had come to see me. He was seated downstairs in the front hall, unimpressive in his black suit with standing collar.

As soon as he saw me, he said, "If I could see Komaki-san's daughter for a minute . . ." I told him that she was not in the house, but he repeated, as if I had hidden her away somewhere, that he just wanted to see her for a short while.

"Tell me, are you suggesting that that the young lady and I have some sort of relationship?" I asked.

A little smile floated up onto his face as he produced another business card from a large folder and placed it in front of me. Tōhō Private Detective Agency and his name were printed on it. "Well, actually, before I came to call on you here," he began, "I asked around in the neighborhood. And as a matter of fact, I myself have seen the young lady standing in front of the train stop nearby once or twice." This was, I gathered, his clumsy way of trying to elicit information from me.

"Why don't you search the house? But you might as well realize that only my wife and I and our child live here." Of course had the woman actually been there, I would have said the same thing. While what this man had to say mattered to me not at all, I did want to know about her activities. "Oh, so she's run away then?"

"About a week ago." He looked at me suspiciously, as if to say there was no point in pretending not to know. "But Yuasa-san, after that night you went with her to the Bōkai Hotel, what exactly happened?"

"The Bōkai Hotel?" I had no problem feigning surprise. "So you've decided that I went there, have you? And what makes you think that, may I ask?"

He told me that after she disappeared they had searched the room and on the floor found a clipping with my picture. The maid said she had left the house in a taxi with some man and after they'd located the taxi and shown the driver my photograph, he identified me as the man with her. At the hotel, the bellboy also definitely identified the man in the photograph as the person who had been with her.

"If the facts weren't already plain as day," he concluded, "I would not have come here like this."

"You do seem to have an unfortunate way of choosing your

words. What do you mean 'facts'?'' I spoke loudly for his benefit. "And who gave you the right to cross-examine me anyway? I don't see any reason why I should have to answer any of your questions. So what if the woman did come here on one occasion?'' Once those words left my lips a wave of anger shot through me. The man thought things over, and either overwhelmed by my aggressiveness or convinced by my explanation, he said he must have been mistaken and left.

So she had run away. She hadn't returned home from the hotel but had gone off somewhere. I bore some responsibility for this, I knew, but frankly I didn't think there was too much to be concerned about. She was, after all, the kind of woman who after seeing a man on the train for a minute goes chasing after him. Bizarre behavior like that rarely brings tragic consequences, I told myself, dismissing the matter from my mind. The next day I went alone to a violin concert at the Imperial Theater and when I walked out to the corridor for a smoke two young ladies approached to ask, "Excuse me, but aren't you Yuasa-san?'' They were both friends of Komaki Takao and they invited me to the coffee shop upstairs to have a talk about her. One of them was nothing special, but I couldn't keep my eyes off the other, a beauty vibrant like a flower that has just bloomed. It was the first time since my return to Japan that my eyes had feasted on such beauty. The cool autumn freshness in her speech and facial expression was definitely not to be found in the women I'd seen on the streets. Her name was Saijō Tsuyuko—the Tsuyuko who was to rule my life, who turned my fate upside down.

I did not behave as I had the day before, losing my temper and denying everything asked me by the private investigator. On the contrary, when they inquired whether I would help search for Takao, I was quick to volunteer my services to aid them in their efforts. "Her poor mother,'' Tsuyuko murmured. Takao's mother had gone out as we had that night but apparently feared that if anyone discovered how negligent she had been in her husband's absence, her comfortable life would be as good as over. It was difficult for me to feel any sympathy for her since my heart was filled with a new excitement. I suspected that great pleasures were in store for me if I joined this beauty, Tsuyuko, in her search for Takao. I had this in mind when I told them that if they needed me they should send a telegram. Then we parted.

Three days later, in the evening, a telegram came from Tsuyuko, asking me to meet her at Tokyo Station the next morning at six. Six —wasn't that just about daybreak? I barely slept and woke up early to rush to Tokyo Station. Tsuyuko was already waiting by herself at the ticket gate. When she saw me she raised her hand high to show me two blue tickets. "Well, our detective work has finally begun," Tsuyuko exclaimed, starting to walk briskly toward the platform. Her frail narrow shoulders just about reached mine.

"Do you know where she is?" I asked.

"Yes." She glanced at me, her dark eyes lit from within. "Yesterday her mother called to say that she's at a hotel in Zushi."

Although the detective agency had discovered Takao's whereabouts, the belief was that if the detective or her mother went after her, she would become even more impossible to manage. Thus, Tsuyuko, as Takao's close friend and confidante, seemed the logical choice.

The early train was empty. "I haven't had anything to eat," I said. As I made do with some bread and coffee I couldn't really believe that the purpose of this pleasant journey was to search for that woman.

The cool morning breeze slipped in through the train window. Tsuyuko began to speak brightly. "I feel I've known you for a long time. You have quite a reputation, you know. Komaki-san would tell me all the gossip about you whenever we met, and on the phone too. She would call me all the time, just to chat."

"That sounds just like her." I was by this time completely captivated by Tsuyuko and didn't want her to get the wrong idea about me from Takao's reports. It seemed wise to make the substance of our relationship clear: "The only thing I can say about that young lady is that I found her quite out of the ordinary. That much I will say."

"Really—? Then taking on a job like this must be an imposition."

"Not at all, because of the chance to be with you . . ." At that point I would have said anything to win her over.

When the train arrived at our destination, we took a taxi to the hotel but progress at the front desk was slow. There was no guest registered as Komaki Takao, because of course she must have used a different name. And even after we carefully described her, the clerk did not immediately say that he knew the person we were talking about. With six or seven young women staying there, he couldn't say which was Komaki-san. We didn't know what to do next.

"Why don't we go down to the beach?" I suggested. "She might have gone out for some exercise."

From the terrace of the hotel we went out to a wide lawn leading down to the sea. Soon Tsuyuko stopped short to exclaim, "There she is!" Takao was noisily playing ball with some Western children. She looked like a child herself in her short dress and loosely hanging hair. We simply stood there, dumbfounded at coming upon her, although we should not have been surprised because her behavior was entirely in character.

"Don't throw it there!" she cried, chasing after the ball like a puppy. Suddenly she looked up and recognized us. Her eyes seemed to widen and flash blue for an instant. Then she abruptly threw the ball down and without a glance our way, passed by to go rapidly up the stairs.

"I wonder why she did that?" Tsuyuko said. "I suppose it's because I came with you."

"Nonsense."

We went chasing after her. Once I made up my mind to follow I wouldn't stop until I caught up with her. She turned down several hallways and entered a room facing the sea. We didn't hesitate to fling open the door.

"I know all about you two coming here." She'd spoken after a brief silence, saving her scorn for those oddly rude words "you two." Here was a woman who had shared a bed with me for a night and who was an old friend of Tsuyuko's, and now she looked at us with eyes flashing hostility and hatred.

Tsuyuko spoke to her softly. "But it was only last night we decided to come. Yuasa-san traveled all the way out here just beause I asked him to. Don't you think it's impolite to talk that way?"

"I know all about it," she repeated more stubbornly. Then, turning her back to us, she let out with a man's whistle through the open window.

"Maybe I should leave?" Tsuyuko asked quietly. She must have thought that Takao's ill temper was a result of my coming with her, for she wouldn't listen to me when I tried to stop her from leaving the room.

Left alone, I couldn't do much but light a cigarette while Takao kept her back to me and waved down to the sea from the window. She seemed to be signaling to the children she had been playing with, and perhaps she also wanted to irritate me.

"What are you so angry about?" Then I collected my wits enough to ask, "You came here right after that morning, didn't you?"

"After being insulted like that another woman would have killed herself." She spoke to me for the first time.

"Insulted? I insulted you?"

"Could there be any worse insult than to be left in some hotel room like that?"

"You must be joking. You're the one who brought me there. You said that yourself that night. And what happened that morning, believe me, it's not as you're imagining it. I didn't run off and leave you. I kept calling to you but you wouldn't wake up." It may be hard to believe but the truth was I almost never went off and stayed with a woman overnight. Even when I was abroad without my wife, I always returned to my own place at night. This was nothing more than an old habit, but it was one reason I didn't want to stay on in that hotel to linger beside her until she got up. "And besides, I had some very important work to do—" I was just adding this when someone interrupted me.

"Komaki-san! Komaki-san!" A young man who looked like a high school student came running in. "I'm all ready, so hurry up. Oh, I see, you have a guest?"

"It's all right," she told him. "I'm coming. Wait a minute."

She hid herself behind the curtain partitioning the room and soon emerged in a white summer uniform. Then, without so much as a glance in my direction, the two held hands and skipped down the corridor. I had to wonder about that childlike young man in the white sports shirt, since she must have been calling him when she whistled and waved out the window. But realizing that we hadn't discussed any of the important issues, I hurried to the entranceway downstairs where Tsuyuko was waiting. Together we followed after Takao and the young man, but they were so far ahead on the beach that there was little chance we'd be able to catch up. From where we were on the lawn, we could see a boat with a red sail being untied from its mooring. They quickly got in and pushed off into the water. As the boat ran full sail with the wind, all we could do was stand there astonished while they traveled further away.

"Well, she's certainly managed to outmaneuver us. What shall we do? Shall we wait it out here until they come back?"

"I suppose so," Tsuyuko answered wearily.

"Why don't we rest over there?" I put my hand on her back and guided her to the terrace, where there were some chairs to sit on.

Before us, the blue sea spread out wide under a clear sky and off in one direction we could see Shōnan's waters. The movement of the red sail seemed to mock us as it went back and forth, riding upon the blue playground of the open sea. But then again, it could have been just an innocent outing on the boat. "What a funny sight," I observed in a cheerful voice. Until that moment Takao's flight from home had taken on the dimensions of a tragedy in my mind, but now, thanks to Tsuyuko, I found I could laugh it off. For a man sitting beneath the bright summer sky with the sea breeze blowing as he talks with a beautiful young lady, gloomy thoughts are simply not possible.

Gaiety filled me and, while this might have all been in my mind, Tsuyuko also appeared to brighten. "It almost seems funny," she declared, "the way we were so upset before. She really refuses to let things bother her— I suppose it's a little disappointing."

"But think of it—if it hadn't been for her we never would have met. Frankly, I'd be grateful to her if she ran away from home all the time."

She laughed. "But that boat is wonderful, isn't it?"

"They know what they're doing and it doesn't look as if they're coming back. What do you think? I know it's early but do you want some lunch?"

After we had eaten, we went walking in a nearby pine grove. By then I didn't care in the slightest about where the boat had gone. My concern over Takao's fate had long since vanished, and as we took our leisurely stroll I began to imagine that I had come to the seaside with the woman I loved. But Tsuyuko looked up once we were back at the hotel and saw that they had returned. We could see Takao in her slip standing by a second floor window that looked out on the sea. She was doing an exercise that involved stretching rubber bands with her hands. Though it wasn't with the same sense of urgency as before, we climbed the stairs quickly and opened the door without knocking. Takao turned around. The informality of her attire did not bother us.

"How could you run off like that when we've come all the way from Tokyo to see you?" Tsuyuko reproved her gently. "You could at least invite us in for some tea."

"Please help yourself. I don't see how you can complain about me when you two come rudely barging into my room without any warning." Takao's expression was hard and unmoving, like a stone.

"Do you mean that? Takao—" After some time Tsuyuko continued, "You're getting angry like this because of a misunderstanding."

"Misunderstanding, did you say? What makes you think I have you two on my mind?" A shadow of a smile floated across Takao's thin lips.

We could hear someone singing happily from behind the partition curtain and in a while the young man Takao had gone off with came out, drying his wet hair in a bath towel. He must have taken a bath upon their return from sailing, but now he stood there so startled that he suddenly turned red.

"Don't worry about them, Tamotsu-san. I want to introduce you. Come over here." Takao spoke to him as if issuing an order. Then she told us his name. "This is Ataka Tamotsu. He's my boyfriend."

I found out later that this young man had met Takao on the second day of her stay at the hotel and from then on they had lived together. He later committed suicide because of this love affair—this student at Keiō's preparatory school, barely eighteen, with beautiful eyes like a woman's. Although we had no choice but to speak to him courteously, it was clear by then that Tsuyuko and I were completely superfluous.

"Takao," I began, "I hope you don't think that we've come here on a lark. I don't know what your plans are, but why don't we have a talk and come to some agreement about going back together? You can always return here later on, perhaps even tonight . . ."

"No. You're just wasting your time coming out here to get me. Tell that to my mother. I'm tired of people telling me to do this for my mother's sake, or do that for the family's sake. When I get good and ready, I won't have any trouble finding my own way home."

Hearing her speak like that made me see how ridiculous our position was, since she was going to do just what she wanted.

"Tsuyuko," I murmured, "could you come here for a minute?" We both went down to the office in the front hallway. After a brief conversation we decided that we would call the Komaki house in Tokyo and tell them about what had gone on since morning. We would leave their daughter there for the time being and return to Tokyo, since in our opinion the problem was not very serious.

. . .

Soon after that episode I read about the financial collapse of Takao's family in the morning newspaper. The paper was full of the Taiwan Bank panic and the ruin of Komaki Yoshirō, a shrewd entrepreneur in the financial world with close ties to powerful men in banking. The reporters had something of a field day since they couldn't have asked for a better human interest story. They had obviously tracked down every scintilla of gossip about how Takao's father had ridden on the tides of prosperity and, backed by influential figures, had speculated on iron and rice, amassing a huge fortune almost overnight. The man had clearly been clever about making good use of a promising economic situation and had diversified his undertakings, but his empire had been swept away in the recent international economic slump. He had struggled for a time, looking for a way to salvage things, but then there had been the panic at the bank. Apparently this had been the decisive blow and bankruptcy his only recourse. I held the newspaper in front of me for a long time while trying to keep my emotions under control.

One day I was actually wondering about what had happened to

Takao when a middle-aged man who was obviously from a good family came to see me. He was the older brother of that young man I had met at the hotel in Zushi. He started out by apologizing for being so blunt but told me that soon after I'd seen Takao, she had left the young man in the hotel and returned to Tokyo. She had promised to come back that same day but she hadn't returned to the hotel, nor had she written or even telephoned. Ataka had no idea where she was but finally it occurred to him that she had left him for good. The idea of a rejection had been too much for him. He wrote a will and was about to take a lethal drug when, as luck would have it, his older brother had come for him. They returned to Tokyo but his state of mind had deteriorated so much that he couldn't be left alone at all. The man went on to say that he couldn't understand what had driven his younger brother to act that way, but then he had found out that I—and here he pointed at me—knew quite a bit about Takao. He would deeply appreciate it, he said, if I would go to see her and, for the boy's sake, find out what her feelings were. To tell the truth, I had had enough of Takao but I was moved by this man's gentleness and by the memory of the way his younger brother had flushed that day, like a child. And yet what could anyone hope to achieve for this love affair which was obviously headed for tragedy?

I tried to console my guest. "But tell me, did you read the newspaper article a few days ago about the Komaki bankruptcy?"

"Yes, I read it." The man bent forward slightly. "I did read it, and I know this may sound rude, but now perhaps she might just agree to a marriage . . ." He said he felt awkward talking like this, but his family back home was an old one, rather well known in Shikoku, and they intended to do their best to establish a secure future for Takao.

His last words made me decide to discuss the matter with her and I left the house with my guest to set off immediately for the Komaki residence in Sendagaya. The front gate was nailed tightly shut and the name plate had been stripped away, leaving an empty hollow. I opened the back gate, where I had taken the taxi with Takao that night, and the young maid I had seen before came hurrying out. I explained why I had come but was told that Takao and her mother were not there. The father, it seemed, had long since gone on a trip and had not come back. Inside the house the lawyers were going through the papers. I stood there for a few moments in a quandary. "Now what am I supposed to do?" Hearing me muttering, the maid, who probably misunderstood the nature of my relationship with Takao, gave me an address where she said the young lady was staying alone. Close to Sangūbashi Station on the Odawara express line, I eventually located a house on the embankment by the railway crossing. It was the same street address the maid had written, but since there was no name plate I walked back and forth in front of the entrance several times. Was this where Takao was hiding?

Although what I did next was completely out of character, I found myself getting emotional and yelled up to the second floor, "Komaki-san! Komaki-san!" The woman from the adjoining house opened her back door and stuck out her head. "She just went to mail some letters. Why don't you go inside and wait? She'll be back soon."

I did as I was told and opened the gate. Once inside I didn't hesitate to take off my shoes and step up into the house. To my surprise it was empty—there wasn't even a single pillow on the tatami. In the kitchen were leftovers from a meal of Western food that had been delivered, but other than that, not so much as a single rice bowl. I stood in the Japanese-style room wondering if a young woman could actually live alone in this house. On the second floor I found the piano and the large red chair, but seeing how they stood in stark contrast to the general bleakness there, I realized for the first time what expensive items they must have been. Takao still had not returned, so I went downstairs again and leaned against the pillar in the front hall. I waited a long time until I heard her footsteps—then the front door was flung open and she acknowledged me at once. Her eyes remained fixed on me, reeling in shock and alarm, but that was only for an instant. Then she burned with the hate and pride of someone who has been hurt. I actually thought she might hurl herself at me.

"Excuse me," I began, before I even had a chance to collect my thoughts, ". . . for coming in like this while you were out."

Takao answered in a low and trembling voice. "You've come all the way out here to laugh at me, haven't you? Why do you go around chasing people? And who said you could come in here?"

"Actually," I continued, no longer afraid of her sharp tongue, "the woman next door told me I could come in—and I have no intention of laughing at you."

"Get out! Get out of here!" she cried over her shoulder as she went up to the second floor. I went rapidly up after her. I don't know why but I liked that anger in Takao—she was at her most attractive then.

"Get out of here, I said, didn't you hear?" The right side of her upper lip trembled slightly as she glared at me.

"Do you know why I'm here? Ataka is close to death because of you." I was unprepared for the scornful smile that rose to her cheeks as soon as she heard me say Ataka's name. I stopped talking, fascinated by what I saw in that sneer.

"Thanks for all your trouble." She managed an almost inaudible response.

Wondering whom she was addressing, I made myself ask, "What did you say?"

"Thanks for taking all this trouble. Please leave me alone now."

"But why won't you go and see him? Tsuyuko and I thought he seemed like a nice person. It was because you liked him that you arranged for him to stay with you, wasn't it?"

"That's true. But it's over." Takao's eyes blazed defiantly. "We had a good time together on the hotel beach for about a week. But who wouldn't do that? Most people who walk along the beach and see a pretty shell want to pick it up. But you pick it up, walk with it for a while, and then discard it without a thought." Even though she spoke with such aloofness, her face became pale and her expression razor-sharp. "Listen, why are you staring at me like that? You wouldn't do the same? You wouldn't pick up something just for fun? Don't think I'm trying to be mean. It's just that I don't need you meddling in my life."

"But listen . . ." Her reasoning, I decided, was built on a way of dealing with the world that was peculiarly hers. She was the kind of person who would brazenly tell lie after lie even if it went against her own self-interest. I was suddenly seized with pity for such a woman.

I had to give her credit though—she had lost her home and now lived hidden in this place with only her piano and red chair, but in her manner of speech she was more than ever the queen addressing her court. Studying her expression carefully, I used my last trump: "I'm going to talk to you frankly because I know you are a bright young woman. Even if it is as you say, that you picked up a pretty shell you found, that was not an ordinary shell. To put it bluntly, there were many real pearls inside. Do you know that if you agree to marry Ataka, his family will make sure that you have no financial worries for the rest of your life? They say they'll do whatever you want."

"So that's what's happened." She interrupted me with words that pierced like a needle. "You've come to laugh at me just as I thought. You're trying to be kind to me because I'm in trouble and you think you're going to cheer me up. You're a fool, that's what you are."

Suddenly the desire to be mean shot through me as I remembered what she had said to me the night we first met: *How can you paint, living in such a house?* That had been an attempt to suggest the advantages that lay in store if I entered into a relationship with her. What was she thinking? She, who had spoken those words with such utter coolness, was now misinterpreting everything I said, inventing a meaning more unpleasant than what was actually in the words themselves.

"Don't you remember saying a long time ago that you'd make my own life more comfortable and secure?" I found myself seething with anger. "Were you laughing at me then?"

"As a matter of fact, yes. It's natural for someone with money to laugh at someone who doesn't have any. Now please get out! I just won't stand for having the likes of you laughing at me."

"I suppose this is a fight we're having, isn't it? Well, it's all the same to me if I lose this one."

Outside, dusk had almost fallen. I walked quickly for some moments before realizing that Takao had been left on the tatami to cry all alone. But actually, whether she was crying or not, I couldn't have cared less. As I walked along preoccupied with my thoughts I felt only a desire to see Tsuyuko. Since that day at Zushi I had met her a couple of times and before long we had drawn closer to each other. I raced to the red telephone box in front of the station and called Tsuyuko, telling her that I wanted to discuss Takao and would she meet me now at the Eskimo in Ginza. By then I had no more interest in Takao and her haughty tears.

. . .

I had to wait in the Eskimo for only a short while before Tsuyuko arrived with her hair down and wearing a thin white kimono, the very image of a beautiful flower glowing in the flickering street light. I was overjoyed to think that perhaps she'd worn her hair that way because she remembered the time I'd gone to meet her near her house when she had come rushing out from the garden behind with her freshly washed hair still in bunches and hanging down her back. The style was most becoming—so clean and pure that I had told her then that I liked her best in that hairstyle.

"Thank you for coming." Then, while utterly delighted to see her, I proceeded to speak about completely different matters. I told her about the request that Ataka's older brother had made of me, about how I had just gone to see Takao, and how I had been turned down flat and thrown out. Tsuyuko and I always spoke of Takao, but frankly the topic of our conversations hardly mattered. As I talked, I could only see Tsuyuko's eyes and lips, her white forehead faintly moist with perspiration, and the slender hand holding her handkerchief. "I tumbled out of the entrance like a ball . . ."

"I knew all along you didn't have a chance," Tsuyuko smiled. She believed that the Komaki family's ruin would make Takao feel insulted no matter what proposal she received. Had Takao been lying and in fact actually loved Ataka, she still would have rejected my suggestions. "If you had asked me first," she declared, "I wouldn't have let you be their messenger."

"I looked like a fool, didn't I? But since she acts so arrogantly and refuses to get married, I really wonder what she intends to do."

"Are you worried about her future? She'll be all right." Tsuyuko went on to explain that Takao's father, suspecting that such a day might come, had probably settled a fair amount of the estate on

Takao and her mother. Their lives had been turned upside down by the financial reverses, but apparently their immediate needs could be met. Takao's father, moreover, was unlike most businessmen in his great learning and high principles. In fact, after he had been forced to sever his connections with the business world he had gone to Shanghai to take up scholarly work as a professor at the Ikuei Shoin, a new occupation he had been looking forward to for some time. Tsuyuko told me that the father had been poor when growing up and so the mother's well-established family had adopted him and he had married their daughter. But as of long ago, from the time he first became a Komaki, he and his wife had not been at all happy together and finally had given up trying to create any semblance of a warm family. Eventually both went their separate ways. The mother, who had studied the singing of old ballads of some school or other since her childhood and had received a secret professional name, socialized with Kabuki actors and the like. In addition to the main house in Sendagaya, she had another in Imai-chō in Akasaka. Whenever her husband was away she lived there with an actor she'd known since she first began singing lessons. In a way, the ruin of the family fortune had only settled the manner in which each member chose to live, and matters were not so unfortunate as they appeared. If what Tsuyuko said was true, Takao's future was not so grim as I'd first thought.

In any case, as far as I was concerned the issue of Takao and her situation was only something to discuss while I ate sherbet with Tsuyuko. I decided to telephone Ataka's older brother from there and when I told him that my efforts had ended in failure I could hear him sighing at the other end. He said he wanted to see me anyway, to hear the details, and would take a taxi straight over. I'd been thinking how pleasant it would be to take a walk around Ginza with Tsuyuko and it seemed like an imposition to have to wait for a man in order to have a conversation that would accomplish absolutely nothing. Still I had no choice. He soon came in wearing a haori of thin black silk over his kimono. Once again, in excruciating detail, I recounted my meeting with Takao to him. Frankly, it did my nerves no good at all to see his skinny shoulders heaving up and down as if they were breathing of their own accord.

At last he looked up. "Well, does this mean the only thing left is to stand by and do nothing while my brother dies?"

He was apparently referring to Takao as the one standing around and watching his brother die, but depending on your interpretation, he could also have meant that I was letting the boy die. Was this how a gentle person acted when he lost his temper?

"The poor boy." He spoke as if he blamed me, his messenger. "When he finds out about this, he'll kill himself. There must be something else you can do."

I was really starting to feel quite irritated. By that point, anything he did would have been fine with me and so I suggested that he go over and see Takao himself. All my suggestions she would surely stubbornly reject, but it was entirely possible that he would get better results. The man stood up, looking very dejected. Even so, he went off to meet Takao. It was the end of July and since there'd been only a sparse rainy season that year, a choking humidity enveloped the night. By the time Tsuyuko and I stepped outside the Eskimo we were no longer thinking of anyone else.

After that, Tsuyuko and I kept meeting every so often. We would walk aimlessly downtown, drink tea, and then part, but each time our feelings deepened. At first I seemed to be playing in love's tournament without a partner but gradually I came to believe that Tsuyuko might also have become a participant. Once, looking very grave, she asked me to honestly describe my feelings for Takao, whom she had just seen the day before. Takao had talked about me, all the while jeering at Tsuyuko: "I'm still planning to marry that man. You'd better keep that in mind." Although Tsuyuko was sure she understood the motives behind these outbursts, she wanted to know whether my relationship with Takao still merited such remarks. Of course, the gist of Takao's claims hardly mattered to me, but I was delighted that Tsuyuko had responded like a jealous lover. "Typical of her to talk like that," I said, thinking how much selfish, spoiled girls delight in bewildering others. I explained to Tsuyuko that Takao had offered those words as a parting shot and was not to be taken seriously. So great was my love for Tsuyuko in that moment that I would have given anything to have drawn her slender shoulders closer to me as we walked side by side.

. . .

Four or five days later I received a telegram from Tsuyuko saying that an urgent matter had come up and would I please go to Takao's house in Sangūbashi. Some more trouble Takao's cooked up, I thought, but since it would give me the chance to see Tsuyuko, I of course decided to go. There was no wind that day and as I walked in the blazing hot midday sun, seeing Tsuyuko was the only thing on my mind.

"Anyone home?" I called out, but no one answered. Although there weren't any sounds coming from within the house, I recognized Tsuyuko's black velvet sandals in the entrance and quickly went up to the second floor.

"What happened?" I asked.

"Forgive me for asking you here," Tsuyuko began. Takao had thrown herself on the piano seat and was crying.

"What happened?"

Tsuyuko picked up a letter that had been tossed aside on the tatami and showed it to me. "Ataka-san is dead."

I was stunned. Ataka had kept insisting he wanted to die, but I hadn't thought that he would die so easily. So he had done it after all. The letter was from his older brother and had been written to Takao. While I was reading it, the strange irritation I'd felt for him since the time we'd met at the Eskimo gradually disappeared. "Now that this has happened, I feel no desire to blame anyone," was the tone he took in the letter. He wrote in detail about what had occurred after he left us:

> I was completely exhausted from keeping watch on him day and night and so I thought that if we sent him on a trip he would stop being so preoccupied with his troubles. We decided to send him back to our parents in the country. But during the trip he threw himself off the boat en route to Shikoku. There was a strong wind that night and my wife, who was accompanying him, had left him for only about thirty seconds to go back to her room to get a cape for him. It was in that brief moment that he disappeared. She says she heard the sound of the water when he

29

jumped and others say that they actually saw a dark figure leaping into the sea. His body has not yet been found. . . .

I put the letter down and looked at Takao, who was sobbing, her shoulders heaving. So even she could cry upon realizing that a young man had killed himself for her.

I felt sorry for her. "Stop crying. It'll be all right. Soon everyone will forget all about it." She made no reply and kept on sobbing. "Come now," I continued to urge her, "you must get hold of yourself. There's no sense making yourself sick over this."

The crying ceased in the stillness that followed. Takao suddenly looked up, trembling with deep emotion as she stared at me, her large eyes washed with tears and her eyelids swollen like pink shells. Then, unexpectedly, the shadow of a sneer flitted across her face as she began to speak. "You've got it all wrong. I'm not crying because he is dead."

Surprised, I averted my eyes. With this latest demonstration of a "spoiled young lady's perversity" she had managed to extinguish any feeling of sympathy that might have been aroused in me. What did it matter to me that she was crying? Seeing me fall so silent and sullen, she tried to pick a fight. "You know, the other day when his brother came to see me, I explained the situation very clearly. I told him it was stupid to send Yuasa-san as a messenger—that perhaps he wasn't aware of it, but Yuasa-san is my lover. I told him it was completely idiotic to send my lover to negotiate about some other love affair."

I was shocked. What would she say next? Great turmoil surged through my heart even though I realized she was only trying to make us squirm. Tsuyuko, who had been listening nervously, scarcely able to sit still, stole a glance at me as if to seek help.

I shouted at Takao. "Stop talking nonsense!"

"Nonsense, did you say? Can you honestly say you're not my lover? Can you say it out loud right here in front of Tsuyuko? We've never really said good-bye to each other. Isn't that true? If we're not lovers, why then did we go to a hotel together? We slept together in the same bed, didn't we?" She let out with mad, loud laughter.

"What are you saying? Can you tell me what good all this nonsense does?"

Although I hadn't been trying to conceal the episode, I hadn't yet spoken to Tsuyuko about the night in the Bōkai Hotel. Thus the words that came pouring out of Takao's mouth must have sounded more ominous to Tsuyuko, who didn't know the real facts. At that point, of course, there was no way I could explain everything to Tsuyuko, and having finally understood why Takao had summoned us there, I was more distraught than angry. Tsuyuko had recently come closer to me but there was no telling how her feelings would change after hearing those words. I had fallen right into Takao's trap and could only blame myself for becoming so agitated.

"That night, as you well know," I continued, flustered, "the circumstances were not so clear as you make them out to be. You completely ignored what was going on in my mind at the time."

At that Takao laughed even more raucously, as if to drown me out. By then even if I used every clever phrase in the book, whatever I said would only have made my predicament worse. I saw that Tsuyuko had quietly covered her face with her handkerchief and was crying silently. At a loss, I took her hand. "Please don't get the wrong idea. The reason I didn't tell you about this was because I was afraid you'd misunderstand. Believe me, it's not at all as she says."

"I know that," Tsuyuko whispered. She buried her face more deeply and continued to sob.

Takao's laugh sounded still more crazed. "Be sure to explain it to her more clearly! Do you have any other excuses you'd like to share with her? I actually had Tsuyuko come here today so we could make a clean breast of our relationship and settle matters between us, but now it all seems so stupid. As of today, I'll have nothing more to do with you. Here, I'm giving Tsuyuko to you. Now, please, both of you, get out! Just get out!"

"Tsuyuko." I forced myself to sound calm. "Let's go."

Tsuyuko was silent as she put her handkerchief in her kimono sleeve and followed me out. We ran down the stairs and out onto the street.

"You're angry, aren't you?" I asked.

"No." Tsuyuko had stopped crying.

It could have been my imagination but those lovely eyes seemed to pity me for being so flustered. To be absolutely honest, if Takao had not worked herself up into a fainting fit that night, I would have had no qualms at all about sleeping with her. No great fastidiousness on my part had held me back but rather a peculiar anger that came from fatigue. In discussing this with Tsuyuko, however, I would only mention that we had definitely not entered into an intimate relationship: "You did notice that she never said anything explicit about that night, didn't you? It was just that certain special circumstances led us to spend the night together in the same room . . . There was a terrible storm and we couldn't get back."

"It's all right. You don't have to say any more. I don't think anything of it."

"Really? Then from today on you'll forget all about it?"

When at last she smiled and nodded her head, I was immensely relieved. Then the dead Ataka came back into our minds.

"She's a strange woman, isn't she—she doesn't even feel sorry for him."

"She certainly was angry. She can't bear to think that people will blame her now that he's gone and killed himself."

Before we knew it we had passed the Sangūbashi Station and come out on an unfamiliar country road. After that episode I did not see Takao again, nor did I have time to think about her. I was completely wrapped up in my love for Tsuyuko, which every moment grew fiercer like a flame put to oiled paper. But from time to time I would hear from Tsuyuko about her activities—how Takao's father had left his wife and daughter and gone to China, and how Takao had apparently joined forces with a competent, energetic young man—a former employee of her father's during his prosperous years—and begun a business importing Shanghai hen's eggs. Nowadays such eggs are sold everywhere, but it was Takao's idea to start importing them in large quantities to Japan. She probably inherited those shrewd entrepreneurial instincts from her father. In any event, she put her eccentric behavior behind her, worked hard, and became quite successful, or so I heard. I assumed that she had married the young man she was working with, but this was evidently not the case. She had become a completely different person. As Tsuyuko explained, "Takao's a textbook case of a split personality." About five years later, this past spring in fact, I saw Takao shopping at a fur store in Ginza. She didn't seem to notice me.

. . .

But to get back to the story of Tsuyuko and me, our love continued to grow in the ordinary way without any complications. I had really been nothing but a boy when I left Japan and I have to confess that during those long years abroad, in a life like mine—where something that passed for love was a necessity—rather than falling in love I had only carried on certain businesslike relationships with women who earned their livings that way. Tsuyuko was the well-brought up daughter of a good family. When she entered my life a foolish, timid love gripped me—a feeling even more childish than the love I had experienced in my youth. And since I was an artist recently returned from abroad, Tsuyuko seemed to have created a girlish fantasy for herself, seeing me as a person from the glittering world glimpsed in newspaper photographs. Into the middle of autumn, the two of us were still behaving like shy lovers.

Such places are probably no longer permitted to operate, but back then there was a restaurant next to Shimbashi Station called the Yū-yūtei. I suppose one could say the guests were all of a good class, but just beyond the entrance, in corners that were dimly lit, there were several small rooms, each with two chairs. Once the curtain was drawn in those rooms, even a person passing by outside couldn't make out who was within. Men would go there with women and those couples would spend the time talking to each other in whispers. Tsuyuko and I often went to one of those rooms at the Yūyūtei —I would take the train from Kamata, Tsuyuko would get on at Yotsuya, and we would meet at Shimbashi. As we talked in the Yūyūtei we could see the dusty leaves of the phoenix trees outside and occasionally we would hear someone playing the piano badly upstairs. The place was practically deserted during the noon hours, and sitting there, we would sometimes be overcome by the quiet misery of lovers who had to hide from the world. After we had met several times in this way, Oyae, one of the women employees, would occasionally come into our room and say, "Well, aren't you having a nice time though?" She teased us like that in the beginning but after she got to know us she would sit herself down, saying, "I know just how you feel," and then regale us with stories about her lover, a movie actor in Kamata. According to Oyae, he had once been a Keiō student but like so many others had fallen into dissolute ways. The money sent to him from home had eventually been cut off, and for a while he and Oyae lived together on her wages. But recently he had started to make a name for himself as an actor—had taken this up to pass the time—and, conveniently forgetting all that Oyae had done for him, rarely came around. "He's very mercenary." Her inevitable sigh was always followed by an offer to help us out if we ever needed it. She often called Tsuyuko's house for me and left messages.

One day Tsuyuko, who was never late, didn't show up. I grew tired of waiting at Shimbashi Station and decided to go to the Yūyū-tei. When I couldn't stand waiting there any longer, I had Oyae call Tsuyuko's house for me but she was unable to get through. Although I was worried, nothing more could be done and I went home. There I found a letter from Tsuyuko on my desk.

> Something urgent has come up that I must discuss with you. Come and wait outside my house tonight after 11:00 p.m. It doesn't look as if I can get out.

All sorts of terrible calamities ran through my mind, but until I met Tsuyuko that night I knew there was nothing I could do. Even so, my heart didn't stop pounding for an instant while I waited for eleven o'clock to come. I went the back way from Shinanomachi Station, down a gently sloping hill to Tsuyuko's house. It looked as if everyone was asleep, for beyond the shrubbery in the dark garden all the windows were closed and the house was quiet. I held my wristwatch up to the dim light under the eaves and saw that it was two or three minutes before eleven. Trying not to make any noise, I walked back and forth in front of the house until I saw a light go on in a room to the side of the entrance hall that must have been the parlor. When the curtain moved slightly I could clearly make out someone resembling Tsuyuko who was apparently trying to be sure that it was me standing out there—in order to make myself inconspicuous I had worn a black suit, not my usual style. Worried that Tsuyuko might not recognize me, I turned toward the figure inside and raised my hand. The figure pointed repeatedly toward the back of the garden as if to say, "Come around there." I made my way along a high brick wall to the back of the house where the thin iron bolt on the wooden door was unlatched. I squeezed my body through the opening and heard only the faint ringing of what must have been a wind chime as I entered the garden.

The light in the parlor went out and Tsuyuko made a nimble jump from the window into the garden. I held my breath, waiting motionless by the shrubbery. Tsuyuko quietly ran over and I could hear her soft sigh as she came up beside me.

I gently embraced her slender body. "What's happened?"

"Something terrible. They're going to make me get married."

"Married?"

Although all was obscured in the deep blackness of night I could feel Tsuyuko's large eyes shining, wild and agitated. I kept her in my embrace as we quietly sat down on a bench near a tree. Meeting her like that, it was impossible for me to take in the seriousness of her news. "I'll never let you get married!" I embraced her firmly once again. Tsuyuko had been a vague white mass from the parlor window but as my eyes grew accustomed to the dark I could see that she looked like a Chinese girl with light peach-colored pajamas and red slippers on her small feet.

"But it's decided," she explained. "Nobody said anything to me while they were all rushing to arrange it secretly."

Her father, an admiral in the navy, had never told her about a decision he had made long ago regarding a young junior officer who was to be her husband. Suddenly that morning she had been informed that the next day she would have a formal meeting with this man at the Kabuki Theater and that she should prepare herself accordingly. "They may have found out about us," she said. "My old servant told me that. So my father is even more determined not to ask my opinion." Although she'd had to accustom herself to living in the coldness of a military home, she sighed deeply, unable to bear the thought that soon she would be leaving her father's house only to find herself in yet another military home. "Help me, please. Don't let them marry me off like this! Please don't!"

She clung to me with a look of terror in her eyes. Her objections seemed to have nothing to do with my being her lover or that the man she would meet the next day was the kind of person she couldn't tolerate in a husband. What seemed to repel her, what made her shudder, was the very thought of marrying a military man. No plan was too drastic if she could escape the next day's meeting. She begged me to find a way for her to get out of it. Now, even supposing that I was ready to die for our love, in the eyes of the world I was after all a married man with a child. How could I ever declare myself as Tsuyuko's lover? Even if my divorce were settled immediately and my child's future made secure, if, above and beyond that, I couldn't tell Tsuyuko's father that I was a fine upstanding member of society with the economic means to secure at least a middle-class life for us, he'd simply laugh me out of the room. I couldn't decide what I was supposed to do.

Seeing me grope for a response, Tsuyuko said, "I have a good idea. Why don't you come tomorrow too? You'll come, won't you? I won't stand a chance if I have to fight my father all alone, but if someone else is with me I won't give in . . . It'll be interesting."

"You're going to upset the arrangements? Is it all right for you to do that?"

"It's fine with me."

When I embraced Tsuyuko once again, her soft, slender body felt so helpless and fragile, reminding me of the times I had held a little baby. "I'll see you tomorrow then."

"Good night."

She drew away and raised her body up into the house like a bird in flight, vanishing beyond the parlor window. I stood by the shrubbery for a long while, looking up to see whether I could tell which room was her bedroom. I waited for a light to go on but the house remained dark and all was finally quiet. I finally went home, much relieved.

. . .

The next day I was careful to go to the Kabuki Theater at just the right time. No sooner had I set foot in that dim hall than, as if drawn by some force, I spotted Tsuyuko and her party. They were sitting in one row to the right side of the stage. There were four people—Tsuyuko, two women of about forty who must have been her mother or her aunt and the go-between, and the man she was meeting. When I saw the four of them watching the play with such an air of composure about them, I was relieved to be sitting far behind. But at the same time, from that vantage point I carefully studied the appearance of the man you could say was my rival. They were obviously complete opposites—the naval lieutenant, who looked like a boor, all rigged out in his dress uniform, and Tsuyuko, with the graceful charm of a white lily just come into flower. I remembered how Tsuyuko had pleaded with me the night before: *Don't let them marry me off like this! Please don't!* It seemed that even then, with her back toward me, Tsuyuko was saying this. I quietly left my seat, approaching them from the rear. The actors were up to the part where the heroine, Okaru, was going off with her lover or something, but I wasn't the slightest bit interested in watching. I was only grateful that the stage lights were helping me get through the dark spaces between the seats as I advanced. Tsuyuko turned around, surprised, but once she recognized me she slipped out and went to the lobby.

"Is one of the women your mother?" I asked.

"It's my aunt and the wife of one of my father's friends. She's the go-between." Tsuyuko was almost giggling.

This wasn't exactly the reaction I'd expected, but I was pleased not to see the somberness that had been in her eyes the previous night. A new lightness of heart made me tell myself that this was just a merry prank that would have a harmless conclusion. I even let myself believe that I was only playing a supporting role in an evening's comedy.

"What should we do? Shall we just run out on the honorable son-in-law and go somewhere?"

"Let's just sit here. Until my aunt comes out and discovers you . . ." Tsuyuko laughed mischievously, moving her body closer to mine.

The bell announcing the intermission sounded and people came crowding into the hall. Just as we expected, a woman who must have been Tsuyuko's aunt elbowed her way through the throngs toward us. "Oh dear, so you're out here," she said, "Isn't it impolite to your guest?"

"It's just that I'm feeling so tired." Tsuyuko edged closer to me, raising her eyes and giving me a significant look. "I met a friend of mine and we started talking."

"You know very well what we've come here for tonight. Please think a little about my feelings too." The aunt spoke in a hushed and controlled tone. Then she turned a hard, smiling face to me. "Please excuse us. I know I am being rather rude but we have a guest waiting for us inside."

She put a hand on Tsuyuko's arm and with a slight pull got her to her feet. I watched them from the back as they went off together. What was I expected to do now? Having come so far, was I just supposed to watch them go, sitting on my hands? Or was I supposed to proclaim, "I am absolutely opposed to having Tsuyuko married off like this"? Should I chase after her and do as Tsuyuko had done before, nestling up close as if to say, "Wherever Tsuyuko goes, I will be right by her side," and completely ruining today's meeting with her proposed husband? I couldn't make up my mind. More than that, I was worried about the aunt who had seen me playing my part in Tsuyuko's drama. What steps might she take with Tsuyuko? Would they, without further ado, decide the whole matter that night or would they give up on the idea, fearing the worst? No matter, I had gained at least some consolation from the assurance that Tsuyuko was not at all delighted about this meeting with the naval lieutenant. Beyond the door I could hear the actors' speeches but they tended to blur into one another as the voices reverberated from one wall to the next. The corner where Tsuyuko and her party were sitting was my only concern. I had to restrain myself from going up there again and with great effort held my ground, standing still for a long while. Finally I decided to take myself home and returned to my seat to get my hat.

When I went out into the hall, Tsuyuko was standing outside the door, her face pale. "Let's go quickly. I slipped out again." She ran out of the theater and hailed a cab that was fortunately passing by. She jumped in and I followed after her. "Shimbashi," Tsuyuko told the driver and broke into a smile. "Let's go to the usual place, what do you think? I was almost tempted to stick it out, but . . ."

"Your hairpin is falling out." It was all I could say. Joy surged up within me as I looked at the white rose ornament in her hair. "Tonight you seem to have become a totally different young lady."

"Just exactly like Takao, wouldn't you say? My aunt was so suspicious that I felt like doing something outrageous to shock her."

Never having seen Tsuyuko behave like a high-spirited, mischievous child, I was swept along by the mood she had created. Even the thought of the dismay we were doubtless causing those people back at the theater began to seem awfully funny.

The Yūyūtei was unusually crowded that night. "What happened? Why are you here so late?" asked Oyae, who seemed a bit drunk as she stuck her head through the curtain. "You look as if you're about to elope."

"Exactly," I replied gaily. "Tonight we've come here because we want your advice." In our small room, Tsuyuko was dressed as beautifully as a bride. I gazed at her adoringly and felt like the young savage who had just snatched the lovely princess, promised as the chieftain's wife, from the wedding ceremony. I sipped some sake. "Do you know some place where we can hide for a while?"

"You're really full of energy, aren't you?" Oyae smirked. Evidently she thought I was only joking. "I've been looking forward to something like this."

She laughed with the same condescension she had shown us in the past when we had been so indecisive, but I put on a serious expression and told her about what had happened that evening. "I'm afraid it's going to look as if I abducted her."

"Oh dear, this isn't good. Not good at all." Her answer was quite unexpected. "Up to now it's been easy sailing, but if you act like this you'll lose everything."

"Don't tell me you're against it?"

"Listen, it comes down to kidnapping a woman, doesn't it? It's a big important family and so I don't think they would dare bring in the police, but don't you think it'd be better if she just went home quietly tonight?"

Even though Oyae was slightly drunk, I had no choice but to consider her advice. Feeling perplexed, I asked Tsuyuko, "How long have we been here?"

"I don't want to go back." Tsuyuko was still smiling. "If I intended to go back, I'd never have escaped in the first place . . . Is that what you want me to do, Jōji?"

"Me?" I stole a glance at Tsuyuko's long eyelashes, fluttering like a feather in the wind. I wondered what, if anything, could ever weaken my resolve never to let go of Tsuyuko. Frankly, my biggest concern was my inability to earn a living. But what could I say to Tsuyuko now? I would have to be as bold as the young savage I'd imagined myself to be earlier. "I won't let her go home even if she wants to. We'll manage somehow. What we need now is a place for tonight." I rose, beckoning Oyae to the corner. "I can't go back on what we've done now. Don't you know any place?"

"There are any number of possibilities all around you. You're the one who should know more about these things than I do."

"But a cheap inn or hotel won't do," I explained in all earnestness. My mind rebelled at the thought of taking Tsuyuko to such places. Besides, I had been living away from Tokyo for quite some time, and the thought of being picked up by the police in a hiding place like that and causing the kind of scandal Oyae had just described really bothered me, so much so it was almost laughable.

"Would you mind if the place is dirty?" she asked me.

"Not at all. By tomorrow, something will turn up."

Oyae wrote a short note for me. In fact, she was offering us her own apartment on the second floor of a house located within the precincts of a temple at the foot of Sendaizaka in Azabu. I thanked her many times and hurried Tsuyuko out of the Yūyūtei. We went directly by taxi to Sendaizaka and when we reached the temple we were surprised at how dark it was. I could not believe a place in town could be so quiet and deserted. Using the map Oyae had drawn for us, we walked through the damp leaves looking for the house.

"You're not sorry about this, are you?" I asked Tsuyuko.

"No." She had left her shawl and kimono coat behind in the theater and her slender, unprotected shoulders seemed chilled.

"I don't like taking you to a place like this."

"Don't even think about it." She had sounded cheerful before but by now her mood had become more subdued.

I walked on, telling myself not to let my courage flag. Finally we located the house Oyae had described and after I produced her note an old lady came out to invite us in. On the second floor were two connecting rooms, one eight mats in size, the other six. We probably shouldn't have expected a waitress's apartment to be any better, but her room was in such a mess that we couldn't even find a place to sit down. The bedding had not been put away that morning and heaps of discarded clothes, scraps of orange peel, and other odds and ends were scattered about. When I opened the window the overhanging branches from the trees outside almost reached into the room as they rustled in the darkness, and a heavy gust of moist air rushed in. I was sure it was pitch dark there even in the daytime. "Just my luck," I muttered to myself. Even the hardiest flower of love would wither in such a bleak room. I of course regretted not having had the courage to go to the Imperial Hotel or the New Grand, since these lodgings did not bode at all well for our future. Realizing that Tsuyuko was probably thinking along similar lines only made me feel more wretched.

"Won't you sit down?"

"All right." Tsuyuko moved toward the edge of the bed and sat down.

"Aren't you cold?"

"No, I'm all right."

"Maybe you want me to take you home?"

When Tsuyuko silently looked at me I noticed a distant coolness on her pale cheeks that I'd never seen before. It was a coolness that seemed to protest the sleaziness of the room even more emphatically —and with that faint chill hovering over us, she whispered her reply. "It's too late now."

I wasn't sure whether she was referring to the time or to the fact that we'd gone too far for her to be able to return home. My despair deepened, and was only made worse by my inability to hold her and kiss her as I always did. I feared we would stay like that until morning. These problems were uppermost in my mind when I heard wooden clogs clattering noisily across the stone pavement outside. With the gradual approach of those clogs also came Oyae's loose, drunken chatter and the hoarse replies of the man she was with. In a few moments they roughly opened the door and immediately came stomping up the stairs.

"Excuse us for spoiling your fun." Oyae, leaning heavily against the man's shoulder, stuck her face into the room. "Yuasa-san, listen. This playboy here with me, he's the heartbreaker I told you about. You just take a look at his face for a minute. He certainly doesn't measure up to you, Yuasa-san—I wish he'd drink something made from your fingernail clippings. Then maybe he'd improve."

"What did you say, you imbecile?" retorted the young man who must have been Oyae's movie actor boyfriend from Kamata. He was wearing a flashy checked overcoat and a hunting cap, and he quickly leered at me. "Excuse her. She's drunk and doesn't know what she's saying."

"Huh!" Oyae piped in and then sank down in a heap on the tatami. "Why are you sitting down there? Oh, I see. If you want bedding, there's another set in the closet. You look as if you've just had a fight."

"Why don't you get the bedding out for them yourself," the actor demanded.

Oyae got up tottering and went into the other room. After she had laid out the bedding for us, she quietly nudged my shoulder. "Why are you sitting around in some kind of daze? Don't tell me you're angry I came back here."

"No, no, it makes absolutely no difference either way."

I tried to sound irritated but finally let the fury stay locked up in my heart. I then urged Tsuyuko into the other room and said good night to Oyae and her friend. Once I had closed the sliding door behind us, the anger within me beat against my heart like great ocean waves. But it soon turned into anger against myself because I knew that even if I stormed out to the streets in the middle of the night, I would accomplish nothing. Resigned, I managed to calm Tsuyuko, getting her to lie down on the mattress.

"Can you sleep?"

"No," she replied. We could hear a car being carried up the hill by the wind. Once the car reached the hilltop, those sounds ceased and then I thought I heard loud voices. Had they come to search for Tsuyuko? Beset as I was by such worries, sleep was of course impossible. Then I heard another car stop on top of the hill. Tsuyuko and I lay there like two broken pieces of driftwood, waiting for the end of that unhappy night. It was hardly surprising that our love had dried up completely, particularly as we listened to the cooing of Oyae and her boyfriend, who kept it up almost the whole night, not the slightest bit bothered about being overheard.

With the first morning light we made our way out past the pillows of Oyae and her lover, who were still fast asleep. Tsuyuko had informed me that in the morning she wanted to return to her father's house. I had no objection if that was her wish—I didn't have the heart to hold her back anymore. Tomorrow, the day after tomorrow, or maybe a week from now, I thought, we'll meet again and with new strength and confidence I'll put fresh life into our love.

"Leave me here," she told me by the Shinanomachi bus stop. "I'll go back by myself now." She smiled sweetly for the first time. "Good-bye."

"Good-bye."

Tsuyuko walked for several yards, then stopped and turned around.

"What's the matter?" I asked.

"I'd like you to go back with me, if you don't mind. I've decided I want you to meet my father."

"Your father?" Certainly I could go home with her, meet her father, and apologize for our rash deed. Indeed, if such a meeting would bring Tsuyuko peace of mind, that would be enough reason to make the effort. However, my present circumstances made it impossible for me to ask her father to let us share our future. And so, like an invalid accompanying his nurse, I walked along with Tsuyuko while I elaborated a number of phrases in my mind. I actually had conceived the foolish idea that I would win her father over by my way with words.

"Oh, she's here," Tsuyuko said, pausing. "That's my old servant."

An old woman standing at the back door of her house came toward us in short, quick steps once she recognized Tsuyuko. "Why, Miss, it's you."

"Is my father here?"

"They're all here. It's good that you have come back, very good."

The old woman's tearful eyes devoured Tsuyuko before she turned to me. In her motherly gaze there was a gentle dovelike softness and she made me remember my own mother, whom I had not seen for a long time. The old woman had figured in Tsuyuko's conversations and although I didn't know it at the time, she was Tsuyuko's only ally in the house.

"I'm sorry to have caused you this trouble," Tsuyuko apologized.

"No, no, I just feel sorry when I hear them criticizing you so much. I'm so happy that you've returned. Come in through here. I'll make whatever excuses I can for you." She pulled Tsuyuko by the hand and opened the back door.

She said she would hide Tsuyuko in her room and then peacefully try to smooth things over. She asked me to leave. I no longer had the courage to argue about going in with Tsuyuko. The old woman didn't have to tell me that just showing my face in the middle of the uproar underway inside would be like pouring oil on the fire. Besides, I had faith in this old woman with her gentle, dovelike gaze. Once it was decided that Tsuyuko would go in by herself, I leaned against the red brick wall to watch the two of them disappear inside. "Soon I'll inform you about what has happened," the old woman whispered again, turning to me at the back door. I stood there for a short time as the early morning sun cast its rays at my feet. The mild warmth seeped up through my trousers but I felt so weak inside that I could have collapsed right there on the ground. That's how exhausted I was.

· · ·

I couldn't get myself to do anything but wait in the house for a message from Tsuyuko. Three or four days passed without a word and my nerves gave me no rest over what had befallen her afterwards. I was also concerned about her emotional state after our dismal farewell. Consumed by the thought that we had to see each other, I went to Shibuya Station where I had waited to meet Tsuyuko once or twice on her way to her flower arrangement class in Konno. I futilely waited on the platform the next day and the next at the correct time, until it occurred to me that perhaps serene, ladylike activities like flower arrangement no longer had a place in Tsuyuko's existence. Was she being kept under such strict watch that she couldn't even write me a letter? As I could conceive of no sensible plan of action, I went by her house to have a look around and walked back and forth in front of the gate two or three times. Even if I couldn't locate Tsuyuko I thought I might just find that old servant, and so I stood by the gate, peering through the garden shrubbery. But the house was hushed, as if no one were inside.

I walked away, turning right at the street that ran along the Yotsuya train tracks and again down a narrow alley at the bottom of a hill. This route took me from that quiet row of estates into a crowded tenement and from there I could see into the back of Tsuyuko's house. I stood on that street for some time, staring into the second floor window of the room I had guessed was Tsuyuko's the night we had met. I could see a light shining from within but I couldn't make out any signs of life through the pale blue curtain. A crazy persistence drove me to walk those streets day and night, although I constantly worried that I had been spotted and that they had taken even greater precautions to make sure I couldn't find her. However, my spirits rose one day when I again reached that miserable slum and noticed a house just ahead with a "Room for Rent" sign hanging from the eaves, and a sign in front saying that cardboard boxes were made there. I could rent the second floor of this house, I thought, and without any hesitation walked in and asked to be shown the room, which rented for three yen per month.

"But it's not the kind of place that a gentleman like you would be able to live in." The kindly old woman rose to go up the dimly lit staircase. Once, long ago, the building must have been a farmhouse, for the dark attic had thick beams. There were cardboard boxes everywhere and heaps of paper scattered about made walking difficult.

"But these days, I'd have a hard time finding such an inexpensive room." I opened the window which faced the traffic and could see the second floor of Tsuyuko's house about thirty yards away. I could even see beyond the bamboo to the pebbled driveway that went from the entrance to the gate. I wouldn't have to wander the streets battling the wind. I'd just sit at that window and keep an eye on the second floor room without arousing any suspicions. Once I realized that I'd also know if anyone went in or out of the house, I was so delighted I could have shouted for joy. I immediately completed all the arrangements and from that day on went to camp out there, carrying a small traveling bag with four or five books in it. I would skim the books while keeping a continuous watch on the window beyond. At night I went home to my house, but as soon as I woke up I again made preparations to go out. After about ten days of this, I had only seen an old gentleman who must have been Tsuyuko's father get into his car at precisely nine o'clock and then leave, returning at exactly three, but I hadn't had a glimpse of Tsuyuko, much less picked up any news of her whereabouts.

"Do you know who lives in that two-story Western-style house?" I asked the old woman downstairs.

"That one? It's Saijō-san's. He's an admiral in the navy."

She then described the family and when I asked her about Tsuyuko she told me that she knew the young lady well. As she recalled the bright red hat Tsuyuko always wore on her way to school, I imagined that she was referring to a red beret and let my mind picture Tsuyuko as a young student in her red beret, a totally different person from the woman I knew. Actually, the vision of this younger Tsuyuko became my only consolation. The old woman had no idea if she was at home or not.

One day, having stayed in that second floor room later than usual, I saw a faint light coming from the house across the way. I was closing the storm windows before going home when I heard a piano being played beyond the window. Astonished, I listened intently and heard repetitions of the same passage from a Chopin nocturne.

46

Ah, that must be Tsuyuko! Who else could it be, I thought, trying to quiet my excitement. I couldn't see the piano or the room clearly through the curtain, but my soul called out to Tsuyuko. In those two weeks my resolve had strengthened and by then nothing would have stopped me from finding her. As I waited for the piano playing to cease, I decided that I'd come again the following night, and if I didn't discover anything I'd come the night after that and find a way to call out to the person at the piano.

From the next day I waited until evening to go to the room. I always heard the piano at the same time, but still couldn't identify who was playing. Of the various plans that occurred to me, I decided to concentrate on the back garden wall, which reached into an alley visible from where I was. I knew that if I tried very hard I could squeeze myself in through the gap I'd been aware of for a long time, between the brick wall and the thorny hedge. From there I could get into the Saijō garden where I'd hide under the lighted window until Tsuyuko left the piano, and then I'd tap on the glass. With this decision, my excitement grew steadily until one night I saw that the window curtain that was usually pulled shut was slightly open, letting a shaft of light about six inches wide fall onto the lawn. Not hesitating for a moment, I quickly went down to the alley, through the gap in the hedge, and into the garden, eventually crawling along to the window. It was from this window that Tsuyuko had once come out to see me in the garden, wearing her red slippers. I pressed up against the wall and stopped to catch my breath. When I at last peered into the room through the curtains, I saw that the person playing the piano with such great absorption was not Tsuyuko but a young girl of fifteen or sixteen who resembled her, probably her younger sister. I crawled away from the window until I could squat down in the dark, letting the notes of the piano float out over me. Now why was it that I had sneaked into someone else's garden? As I brooded there, I was barely able to keep myself from going back and tapping on the window to find out about Tsuyuko. That I could even consider such an act, I realized, meant my sense of discretion had totally vanished, and I was afraid to remain in that spot a moment longer. I quickly cut across the garden and returned to the boxmaker's second floor room, where I sprawled on the tatami and stared at the ceiling for a long time while tears ran down the side of my face. The old servant had promised, "Soon I will inform you about what has happened." I wanted to know—even if I could never see Tsuyuko again, I wanted to know the truth. Why hadn't I just tapped on the window decisively? I suppose spending so much time in that cramped, gloomy room had affected my nerves, and I didn't even feel like rousing myself.

Then I heard an argument downstairs, followed by the rough sound of footsteps coming up the stairs. When two men in happi coats burst in and came over to where I was lying, I looked at them in a daze.

"Hey, Kawahara," one of the men shouted at me.

I got up with a start. I remembered using this name to rent the room since I had been afraid to reveal my own. The men bounded forward to grab hold of both my arms.

"We've got business with you. You're coming with us to the police station."

It dawned on me that they were detectives—they'd come to arrest me and I could only come up with the single notion that someone had reported me, that my careful preparations had all been for naught. My stay in the room, my long watch for Tsuyuko, my foray into the garden just now—all these had been discovered. I got to my feet with both arms still gripped tightly by those men.

"What are you saying? What do—"

"Just shut up. If you have anything to say, say it at the station."

Once out on the bright street, I walked along between the two men and could see what a pitiful creature I had become. Only one objective glance was required to make me realize that I was just a hopeless fool who had lost his common sense over a woman. Now I don't care what happens! Such reckless thoughts flew through my mind as I walked. At the Yotsuya police station, all the detectives inspected me simultaneously with the same piercing glance, though each looked and dressed differently.

"Good work. You've done good, hard work." A man, apparently the chief, came into the room and from that distance threw over a sheaf of papers. "Kawahara! You remember these, don't you? You distributed them, didn't you?"

Once I examined the papers it became obvious that they had the wrong person. They had mistaken me for a Kawahara who was involved in radical socialist activities, and I could only absorb this realization with great pleasure, while mustering a hearty laugh. I tried to remain as calm as possible when I told them my real name and profession, explaining that, as they could well imagine, I could not work at home and so had taken to going to the boxmaker's house where the rented room served as my studio.

"But if you were just renting a studio, why did you have to use a false name?"

"There was no particular reason. I just didn't want to use my real name."

In renting the room to keep watch for Tsuyuko there had been no real motive behind my use of a false name. Perhaps it was simply the pride hidden in everyone's heart that had spurred the decision. Although the chief seemed reluctant to believe me, one of the detectives vaguely recalled an artist with my name and he suggested checking the photograph of me which had appeared in the newspapers when I returned from abroad. At last they dug up an old file copy of the newspaper and my story was corroborated. "Why don't you draw a portrait of me as a souvenir?" the detective asked.

When I was released that night, I walked out of the station and a tremendous anger gripped me as soon as I reached the street. I became so furious I wanted to spit. How I cursed myself for the happiness I'd felt when I realized they had mistaken my identity! And what a fool I'd been to actually sketch the portrait he had requested!

. . .

From the next day I stopped going to the second floor of the boxmaker's house. Once I walked out of that police station the oppression that had clung to me like fog completely lifted. I myself had difficulty fathoming the stupidity that had possessed me as recently as the previous day. By then I was convinced that Tsuyuko was definitely not in the Yotsuya house, that she and the old woman were locked up somewhere far away, but I could think of nothing else to do but wait for my next opportunity to locate her. I remained at the mercy of my nerves for four or five days, and stayed shut up at home. Then one night my wife came up to my room on the second floor, saying, "Telegram for you." She tilted her hard, unmoving face toward me and then immediately went downstairs. My wife and I had been living that way for about six months, waiting for our attorney to send the divorce papers. In some ways we had even become used to it. I silently read the telegram:

HAKONE GŌRA TANIGUCHI ESTATE TSUYUKO

That was the entire message. Tsuyuko was telling me where she was! I read it again. Just as I had thought, Tsuyuko was confined in an estate owned by someone named Taniguchi in Gōra. Along with this news came the peculiar conviction that I had known it for some time. As soon as I got up the next morning I would go to meet her, I decided. Settling upon this plan made me forget the long period of suffering I had just endured—it was as if warm, healing waters had been poured over me. "I'll go early tomorrow morning," I whispered to myself, holding the telegram in my hand. Then a fear came into me, constricting my throat like a severe thirst. Had she sent me a telegram so late at night because a new crisis had arisen and she desperately needed me? It was possible that she'd been waiting for a convenient chance to contact me, but suddenly had an emergency on her hands and couldn't wait any longer. I was unable to sit still. I checked my watch, which showed just past eleven, and calculated that if I hurried I could catch the last train to Odawara, which left after midnight. That was all it took—I put on my hat and rushed to Tokyo Station.

At the station a strong wind howled through the night as if ready to tear away the platform roof. After the stop in Yokohama, the wind mixed with the rain, creating a fierce, whipping downpour. By the time I reached Odawara the storm had become severe with floods sweeping across the utter blackness of the city. The agents of the hotels who had come to meet the train all claimed that it was impossible to go to Gōra in that rain. Perhaps they only said it to get me to stay at their hotels, or was I actually mad to insist on going up to the mountains in that violent storm? Still, since my mind was made up, I gave one of the men some money and asked him to get me a taxi. He came back almost immediately with a driver from the garage in front of the station.

"There are no roads," the driver informed me as soon as I explained where I wanted to go. In the morning he might be able to help, but at night it was so dangerous that we'd almost certainly crash. He seemed very unwilling to budge.

"Why don't you take me as far as you can?" Whenever I am intent on an immediate goal I naturally expect that my singlemindedness will stifle all objections. I continued to press him. "Just turn back once the road gives out. You get the car and I'll give you all my money. I'll pay you whatever you say."

"I'll take you, sir—" Another young driver in a raincoat came out of the same garage. "Where in Gōra do you want to go, sir?"

"To the Taniguchi estate."

The young driver went back into the garage and came out with a convertible. I was about to ask whether this car was the only one he had, but I was afraid that if I complained he might not take me. I opened the door and got in, and soon we were driving away. Someone in the garage had probably made him take the worst car they had. As we drove along the muddy road, the rain, like sticks hurled by the squall, pelted my cheeks through the gashes in the convertible top. I put up my coat collar and listened to the wind rising and falling through the dark night. Tree branches were snapping and tree trunks splitting apart. As we approached the mountain, the road turned into a fiercely flowing torrent with huge rocks tumbling down into the muddy waters. "Sir . . ." The driver tried to tell me something but it was impossible to hear him and his words were swallowed up by the wind. I assumed he was trying to get me to give up going any higher.

I shouted at him to continue. "It's all right! Just a little farther!"

"Taniguchi-san's house is the only one on top of the hill. I'll have to stop the car below the cliff."

"I understand. You just go as far as you can. I'll walk the rest of the way."

Perhaps if I had known more about Hakone I might have given

up on going to that mountain, but I had been living abroad for a long time and had never been to the places that most people had visited at least once. Also, I usually react to difficult situations by feeling even more determined to overcome all obstacles, and the raging weather was actually goading me on. The car almost turned over several times driving through piles of fallen rocks and broken branches. Even worse, the torn top on the convertible made a frightening noise as it flapped in the wind, and the rain, mixed with earth and sand, soaked the seats, beating at us from the side. Several times it seemed as if we were going to be buried in the rain. And after a big tree snapped like a pencil and was washed away from the roots, there was a sound, like the very roaring of the earth, which echoed far into the valley.

"Sir, I will only go this far." The driver finally stopped the car.

His face shone like that of a young soldier in the car headlights and the rain streamed down his face as I silently got out. No house lights were visible, but a sharply inclined road in front of us led up a tall cliff. I decided to follow it and climbed for a while until I vaguely made out a house at the top of a steep hill. It was definitely the Taniguchi estate. As I came closer I saw that the house was built in a simple cottage style and was surrounded by a low fence. Suddenly I turned and watched the car's headlights flickering through the darkness as it crawled down the mountain. At the same time I realized that it must be past two in the morning. I used both my hands to fumble along the wooden fence, going around the outside of the estate several times, but of course found no sign of anyone being awake. Since the gate was open, I went into the garden and then managed to make my way through some small pine trees to the rear of the house. I groped along the exterior of the building, still searching, and circled the whole house once or twice, but I hadn't yet been able to catch any glimpse of what might be going on inside. I rested for a while behind a storage shed while the rain pounded like drumbeats against the tall water tank beside me. Only then did I realize that my body, my hat, my coat, my shirt, and my socks were completely soaked. And in that sea of darkness with the astounding, terrifying wind and rain not letting up for a moment, I could only let out several great breaths to rejoice at my safe arrival. I made another round with my chest against the house and discovered a faint light coming from a window hidden by some tall larches.

As I approached the window I gave no thought to who might be inside or what I would say if I actually discovered someone there. Since the moment I had begun my journey at Tokyo Station and during the entire ride while pitching about in the car as it labored up the mountain, my sole preoccupation had been my need to see Tsuyuko—and that need, like a raging hunger inside me, took precedence over all other thoughts. I can't say precisely why, but I sensed that she might be inside and that prospect stirred wild ideas about how I would, despite the rain, shout out to Tsuyuko if she were there, ask her to leave the house, and together we would run away. I pressed my cheek against the window and looked into the room through a small space between the curtains. The light from the small night table lamp helped me see that it was indeed Tsuyuko lying on the bed reading a book with her back to the window.

"Tsuyuko! Tsuyuko! Tsuyuko!" I called to her but I couldn't even hear my own voice as it was carried off in the wind and rain. I ran over to a window close to the bed on the north side and saw Tsuyuko's white hand holding the book, and her cheek, like a child's in profile, as it sank into the pillow. But I couldn't gaze any longer, for I was suddenly drenched by the rain pelting down on the glass. "Tsuyuko! Tsuyuko!" I called again, but of course she didn't get up.

At that moment I heard a loud conversation out on the road beneath the cliff, and gradually some people approached the house. I instinctively flew from the window to hide among the small pine trees behind the house. Small stones and branches whipped up by the wind struck sharply against my face, shoulders, and back, and it seemed wise to just surrender to the rain. I sat very still without breathing while those strangers entered the garden. Four or five men in straw raincoats carrying lanterns and a large black object came near the trees where I was hidden. My heart started to pound. I couldn't understand why they had come there in the middle of the night. Suddenly a tremendous gust of wind blew up and the light from their lamps fluttered, leaving me exposed for a moment in that flash of brightness. I came leaping out from the trees because I

saw immediately that I should present myself before they discovered me.

"What happened?" I asked before they had a chance to ask me
the same question. They were carrying a young man in a raincoat
who appeared to be drunk—his head was lolling forward as if he were
dead.

"He's a fool," one of the men declared, "driving in this rain."

They had been on emergency duty up on the mountain and were
approaching the bridge below when a gruesome roar made them
look up, only to see the cliff give way. At that moment a car dashed
by with its headlights on, got caught up in the falling cliff and turned
over. Although some of the men went running out to help, they
were already too late, for the car had been smashed like a toy and the
driver hurled from it. He was pinned beneath the rocks, almost
dead. He had been rescued finally, and since this Taniguchi estate on
the hilltop was the only place available in the neighborhood, they
had brought him here despite the inconvenience this would cause.

Was it the car I had come in? I was struck with terror as I looked at
the young man's face—and indeed he was so pale that he could have
been a different person, yet he was definitely the driver who had
brought me there. As I remembered the moment we had parted and
how the rain had run down his shining face, I became so overwrought that I forgot my own situation and how I had come creep-
ing into a stranger's garden. Eventually I made some foolish remark
about what a tragedy this was, but since there was no escaping the
conviction that I had killed that man, I couldn't get myself to look
them in the eye. "Who are you anyway?" one man thought to ask.
With a start I regained my composure and at least had the presence
of mind to explain that I lived at some distance and, having lost my
bearings, had at last found my way to this garden. I went on to say
that since it was karma that had brought us to this meeting, I wanted
to help them care for the young man. I spoke these words very
coolly, and fortunately no one doubted my sincerity as I moved
ahead of the men and went around to the entranceway. With the
help of the lanterns, I could see the front of the house, which looked
like a mountain retreat in stone. The sturdy door had been made
from logs.

"Anyone up?" I knocked hard at the door. "Excuse me, is anyone up?"

A faint light went on inside. Evidently someone was awake and had lit a candle. The flickering light approached and when the door opened, a white-haired old man came out, listened to our explanation, and then went back into the house, only to return to invite us in. We were led into a room next to the entrance, apparently a sitting room, large and simply decorated. The injured man was laid on a couch in the corner. They removed his straw raincoat, revealing a jacket of the same khaki color beneath, and his gaiters seemed to indicate membership in the town's youth group. We asked the old man to bring in some firewood and when a fire was started in the fireplace, the flames illumined the wounded man's face. Outside the blood had been washed away by the rain, but in the room I could see it gushing out from a wound at the base of his head. The white of his fractured skull was visible between the torn shreds of flesh.

"We should call the doctor. Do you have a phone?"

"There's no use calling. There won't be any roads, even to Odawara, after an avalanche like that."

Much whispered discussion followed about how there were back roads but they were more dangerous. Even if someone went out to get medical help, the wounded man probably would not survive until the doctor could get there. An old woman, who must have been the wife of the old man, came in bringing towels and cotton cloth, which she placed on his wounds, but they were quickly soaked with blood. I joined the others and set about opening the buttons on his shirt, trying to help remove his clothes. I pried away his shoes, which stuck to his body as hard as plaster, then removed his socks and shuddered at the sight of his feet—white as paper and cold as ice. For a long time, I was in a daze as I stared at that young man's mouth hanging wide open and jerking from spasms, and at his chest heaving fitfully beneath his soiled white shirt. "He's finished," someone muttered. Was this man going to die? Was he going to die like a poor dog, helpless in this strange house where they couldn't even get a doctor? Because he had driven me? The men stopped trying to help him further and an eerie silence ensued while we waited the few moments until he died.

Outside the wind continued to howl and we could hear the crashing trees that formed huge black shadows as they collapsed. The rain washed over the window frames and I started believing I had always been gazing at the wind, the rain, the flames burning in the fireplace, the events in the room. For some moments I became convinced that there could be nothing more natural than for me to be among these people. But then I became cold and a chill ran down my spine as if I had been doused in cold water. I started shivering and heard my teeth chattering. "He's gone." It sounded like the old man's murmur. So this is how it's going to be, I thought. That man is going to die. Gathering every ounce of my strength, I carefully observed the open mouth of the young driver lying on the couch, no longer supported by anyone. When suddenly his head fell forward from the pillow, I had to cover my face with both my hands.

"Grandfather, bring another candle . . ."

"Oh, the poor boy . . ."

While such phrases floated through the air around me, I believe I saw the candle being placed at the dead man's pillow and the small flickering flame. I felt hot, as if my whole body were on fire. Maybe I'll light a candle too, I said to myself, and was lifting my head to request one from the old man when the door to the next room opened and I saw the slender Tsuyuko standing there in a red striped house coat. Then I fainted dead away.

. . .

I had come down with an acute case of pneumonia from being out in the rain for so long. I heard later that I didn't open my eyes for two days. When I did awaken I was lying on a bed near a sunny window, with a doctor in a white coat sitting by my pillow and listening to my chest with a stethoscope: "How are you? Have you come to?" I knew that the doctor had seen me open my eyes and was questioning me, but as I was about to answer, the white of his coat just above me actually seeped across the entire surface of my eyes, making me suddenly so tired that I went back to sleep. About two days passed before I woke up to savor warm sunshine pouring in from the window onto the bed and across the whole room. A child again, sleeping in the sunshine, I saw someone standing before the window, pulling the curtain. I thought it was Tsuyuko. I had seen the bright purple kimono she was wearing on many occasions and tried to smile at her but was very tired and went back to sleep. When I opened my eyes once more and saw Tsuyuko, sitting there as usual, her presence seemed completely natural, as did the sight of myself in that bed.

Tsuyuko looked very serious. "Did you sleep well?"

"This room is nice and warm." I stared at her long eyelashes.

"Oh, no!" Her voice shrill, Tsuyuko flushed scarlet from fear as she leapt up to make sure no one had come in behind her. "You must be quiet! Nobody knows that it's you." And then an old man did hoarsely call out her name several times from another part of the house.

. . .

Tsuyuko quickly left my side and went to the sliding door to answer that distant voice. Then she paused. "Don't say anything." She looked back at me, holding a finger to her lips, and once again called out, "Grandfather, our guest has awakened. He can talk." I found out later that the Taniguchi estate belonged to Tsuyuko's grandparents on her mother's side. After leaving me to return to her house that morning, Tsuyuko had been summarily sent to this place. "Grandfather . . ."

The sound of Tsuyuko's voice gave me a start and I suddenly recalled the night of that savage wind and rain. The memories streaked like lightning through my mind: how I had stolen into the garden unannounced and the men had appeared carrying the wounded driver, how we had all entered the house, trying to help him, and how he had soon died. I'd lost consciousness, driven by panic and guilt, having been out in the rain for so long. A sense of turmoil and confusion swept over me. I suspected that the grandfather she called must have been the old man who had brought firewood, towels, and candles for the wounded driver. It makes no difference what happens—just relax, everything will eventually work out, I thought, forcing myself into calm as I waited. As it turned out, the well-bred old gentleman who came into the room did not resemble the elderly man I had seen before. He had a long white beard and a warm smile.

"Oh, you've come to?" he asked.

"Please forgive me for causing you so much trouble." Barely able to speak, I was aware of the bright sun and the pink color it gave to the old man's slightly drooping eyelids, but I just couldn't lift my eyes.

He put his cold hand on my forehead. "Your temperature seems to have gone down. There hasn't been much we could do to help you way up here in the mountains." He spoke slowly, apparently remembering something when he brought himself to say, "Also we don't know your name and so we've not been able to inform anyone about what has happened. I heard that you live in the mountains a distance from here, but when I made inquiries no one knew anything about you. Of course this was all very sudden and so it's perfectly natural that we are late in getting the facts out. Where is it that you live?"

This was not an interrogation, I told myself, but rather his way of apologizing for not informing anyone of my illness. Feeling more at ease, I remembered how the men who had brought in the driver that night had asked me where I was from. To evade the question, I'd said the first thing that had come into my mind, that I lived farther up the mountain. I couldn't very well stick to that story now and I felt trapped, but was there actually any reason to worry? If they eventually discovered who I was—well, that would be the end of it, I thought, and, deciding to feign ignorance until then, I calmly answered him. "I'm from Tokyo."

"Tokyo? And what is your name?"

This question was perfectly natural but it put me on the spot. Taking in a deep breath, I foolishly replied, "Saijō Sanjirō. I'm a musician." I definitely should not have said "Saijō," since this was Tsuyuko's family name, but it had escaped my lips before I realized what I'd done.

"Saijō-san, is it?" The old man did not look suspicious. "That's curious. We have a close relation with the same name. Well, it must be some 'karmic relation.' In any case, let's send a telegram to your family."

"No—" In my alarm I quickly interrupted him, and blurted out whatever came into my mind, trying to smooth things over by telling him that my family was in a very southern part of Kyūshū and I'd hate to have my parents rush over because of my illness. Also, I went on, since my residence in the city was only temporary—I was studying in Tokyo—four or five days' absence would probably not seem alarming to anyone there. The old man moved on to other matters but then returned to the same subject, asking why I had come so late at night during that terrible storm. He had probably decided to inquire about certain things as soon as I woke up, but I had come to the end of my tether. His questions seemed focused on my background and in struggling for ways to get around answering I had become drenched in sweat and was feeling at a loss for more clever replies. Fortunately, since my fever made me tire quickly, I was able to bury my face in the pillow, in part out of real exhaustion, and close my eyes.

"Grandfather, leave him alone," Tsuyuko urged. "You shouldn't tire him out with your questions when he has just regained consciousness."

"You're right. That was inconsiderate of me."

I heard them talking as I dropped off to sleep. I'd had to rely on Tsuyuko's deft maneuver, but even so it was lucky that my peculiar illness made me slip into sleep so easily.

I woke up the same day at dusk to find Tsuyuko sitting at the head of my bed. Seeing me open my eyes, she whispered, "My grandparents have gone for a walk." They apparently went for a walk at the same time every morning and evening, leaving only the old servant couple in the house. I smiled at Tsuyuko with my eyes to convey all my thoughts and feelings. Bathed in the dim light from the window, the soft eyelashes over her half-opened eyes cast shadows upon her cheeks like the eaves of a building. The play of delicate shadows about her lips and chin were indescribably beautiful. But I still had a fever and my mad starving love for her lay dormant. Only a quiet happiness overflowed in me like water.

"Thank you for what you did before. Does your grandfather know who I am now?"

"No, and I can't understand why he hasn't realized yet. It's quite funny."

Tsuyuko's laughing, playful eyes were enticing. Feeling at ease once more, I entertained wicked thoughts. Of course I'd deceive them all, I told myself, grasping for a way to escape from the guilt and panic that had tormented me while I had been so wracked by fever. To see if this was indeed true, I began questioning Tsuyuko. "Do you know how I got here that night?"

"Yes." Tsuyuko gazed at me with that same playful look as before. "I know. I know about everything."

"Do you know that I was in that car?"

"Yes."

"That the car turned over during the drive back?"

"Yes."

I gradually became bolder, not fully understanding the change in my attitude. Although the misery I had felt about killing that driver should never have left me, by then I felt completely unconcerned. What had happened back there? A fresh burst of daring in my heart convinced me that whether or not the car bringing me over had had an accident on the way back, it was truly no business of mine.

"Why hasn't anyone else realized this? Anyone from the Odawara garage would surely know." The garage people would certainly have remembered me shouting about where I wanted to go, but perhaps my voice had been swallowed up in the storm and only the dead driver had heard me.

Tsuyuko told me that the investigators and people coming for the body had arrived the next morning, but since I had already been carried into another room, no one saw me and no one connected me to that driver. She showed me a page torn from the local paper and I found an article only three lines long in the local news section which said that a certain person from a certain garage had brought a passenger to Gōra in that fierce storm and so on. While I was sleeping the whole matter had been neatly settled. In this house I had become Saijō Sanjirō the musician, a man completely ignorant of the circumstances of the accident. Only God knew about me, I thought, as I raised a shout of joy in my heart. The divine protection of a wicked god had surely helped my love for Tsuyuko escape from peril.

Tsuyuko's grandmother and grandfather often came to visit my sickroom, but they did not try to question me as before and my health gradually improved as if thin sheets of paper were being peeled off, one by one. Tsuyuko usually sat silently at the head of my bed but when the old couple went out for their morning and evening walk we would warily burst into talk, like lovers who had been playing hide and seek. In those moments we became suddenly elated, but because we were so pressed, needing to discuss everything quickly, we spoke of the most urgent matters, particularly our secret flight from that estate.

"It's all grandfather's fault," Tsuyuko complained. "He said he'd do whatever I wanted. But after he brought me here, he just forgot all his promises. I suppose he's afraid of my father. I couldn't wait any longer and sent you that telegram."

With a speed that made my mind reel, I thought ahead to our life together after our escape. But rather than indulge in pleasant daydreams, I was concerned above all that it not end in a repeat of the bitter experience after the Kabuki. We would go to Osaka, because there I had an old friend, the head of a famous revue, who would find me some work. In the worst possible case, I could always play the piano in his orchestra or even become a comedian. And as for my family in Tokyo, I would ask the lawyer to make the final arrangements for my divorce after things calmed down. This final thought, which came with a businesslike air, sprang to my mind only out of a feeling of obligation to Tsuyuko.

Once we had decided to wait until I recovered and was able to walk, Tsuyuko stopped coming to my sickroom so that it would seem as if we rarely spoke to each other. Sometimes I could hear Tsuyuko calling her grandparents from the parlor beyond, or I would catch the sound of her sandals as she walked outside my room. Lying there alone, I could always sense which room Tsuyuko was in. I had never felt so at peace. When I was feeling stronger, I began to practice walking after her grandparents had gone out for their stroll. "Is it all right if I come in?" Tsuyuko would ask, peering in through the partially opened door. Then I would hold on to

Tsuyuko's shoulder with one hand and walk gingerly around the bed. After about five days I was generally able to walk on my own and we decided on the next morning for our escape. According to our plan, Tsuyuko was to wait until the old people went out on their walk; then she would leave first by the mountain road in back and a little later I would take the short cut to the bottom of the cliff, eventually meeting her at the last stop of the bus which went into town. If all went well, our bus would have almost arrived at Oda-wara by the time her grandparents returned. "I'm so nervous," Tsuyuko said, putting both hands on her heart. Reaching out to take her hands from her breast, I gazed at the flower vase which always held a single fresh flower, at the window where the ice bag I had been using until two days previously hung inflated with air, at the larches outside and the far rising sky chiseled by the sparse branches. As my eyes studied the familiar scenery I all at once understood what a great betrayal it was to flee with Tsuyuko.

"Why, even a thief has a better character than I do," I said. "But then I might have done something worse—"

"I wish you wouldn't talk like that."

"But, really, I don't know what lengths I might go to after this . . ."

Although I tried to sound facetious, the words fell flat and my expression must have stiffened, for Tsuyuko pulled her body from me—"They've come back." A bell sounded and a cane clattered across the stones in front, signaling the old couple's return. "Well then, until tomorrow," Tsuyuko murmured, pausing at the door longer than usual. We didn't realize that those words would mark our farewell.

That night I couldn't sleep and in my anxiety about the next day and the events to follow I became even more wide awake. If I didn't sleep I'd probably have a fever the next day, but the more I tried to sleep, the more parched my eyes felt, and then my body, still not fully recovered, responded to suggestion, for I gradually became hot all over. As I lay there on the bed, it seemed as if I were going to rise up and float off. I tried to relax by telling myself that if I couldn't sleep, I couldn't sleep and not to worry over it since sleep was not an absolute necessity. Gradually the light dawned outside and I heard some water being drawn from the tank, probably by the old maid-servant, who had awakened first. I gave up trying to sleep and decided to make myself comfortable, at least until the time came. I lay there in absolute quiet. Soon it was almost eight o'clock, the time we had decided upon, and I got out of bed and went to sit on the chair. But I couldn't remain still from worry. Was Tsuyuko just then stealing out the back door and hurrying down the mountain path, or was she already at the bus stop with her small suitcase, waiting for me?

Rising quietly, I went to the bureau to take out my socks and the shirt that had been washed and put away. When I started dressing I didn't feel as sick as I had feared. I checked outside for a moment, saw that no one was there, and went to put my shoes on in the entrance. I walked from the sunroom to the veranda, intending to step down into the garden, but suddenly, perhaps because I had gone out onto that bright sunny veranda, I became dizzy and tripped, falling down in a heap on the brick floor. The maidservant had by then come in through the back door carrying a Western-style vegetable basket; she had probably just returned from her morning shopping. As the dizziness overcame me, I saw her run over, shouting—"Oh, Saijō-san, you've got your shoes on." This is the end, I thought. They've found me. Cold sweat began pouring from both my armpits and I lost consciousness.

. . .

When I came to I was back in bed in the same room as before, my mind in a state of confusion and filled only with garbled thoughts about the morning's fiasco. I was there but what had happened to Tsuyuko? I tried to get my bearings by listening for sounds from the other rooms, but perhaps reflecting the feverish state of my imagination, I couldn't hear anyone.

Soon the door squeaked open to reveal the old maidservant coming to stand beside my bed and smiling weakly. "Have you awakened?"

"Yes."

I said nothing after that, waiting for her to explain or for Tsuyuko herself to appear. But while the servant came to my room from time to time to look after me in many kind ways, she always avoided the topic I most wanted to discuss. Tsuyuko, whom I kept expecting, did not come at all, nor did I hear the coughing of the old man who used to talk to me sometimes through the window as he tended the garden morning and evening. Soon I couldn't bear the suspense any longer and asked the servant about Tsuyuko.

"The young lady went back to Tokyo with her grandparents that day around noon."

Only she, her husband, and I remained on the estate. Tsuyuko had gone back to Tokyo that day around noon? Then she had been handed over to her father . . . My strength gone, I closed my eyes while the servant tried to console me.

"But don't worry, any day now a friend of yours from Tokyo will be coming to get you."

"A friend?"

"Yes. A friend of yours will be coming. As soon as you get well, you'll be able to go home with him."

A friend was coming to get me? I didn't know what she meant, although I of course realized that much had transpired while I lay unconscious. They know everything, I thought, and gave up my fight in the unbearable chill of that big silent house. I wanted to return to Tokyo as quickly as possible. I felt I'd fallen naked into a ravine and could find no escape from the gloom that enveloped me for several days. But my body gradually got stronger, in complete contrast to my bleak mood. We should have waited a few more days before trying to flee, I thought, at least until I had recovered to this extent—then, even if I had lost a night's sleep, I might have avoided such an ignominious failure. It gave me no pleasure to look at the walking stick I had taken out that morning, which was resting against the footboard of my bed as if the whole episode were part of the distant past.

One morning I was surprised to hear a car stop on the road beneath the cliff and further shocked when a small man formally dressed in a hakama was led into my room by the servant. This was my senior colleague and old friend, the artist Kusumoto. My mind had barely formulated the question of what Kusumoto was doing there when the answer became clear to me, and I understood that more had been discovered by Tsuyuko's family than I had imagined.

"Hello!" Kusumoto's friendly smile was his most memorable trait and he brought it forth as he looked at me, even then laughing sheepishly at himself for coming in such formal clothing. What a friendly, warm smile! In an instant my gloom vanished and I returned his greeting.

"So how are things?" he asked, opening the window and looking out at the scenery. "I'm glad you got better so fast. What a nice place. I'd like to relax here for two or three days myself." Then he whispered in my ear. "What do you think? What about going back to Tokyo with me? In about an hour there's a car coming to pick us up."

So at last we left the estate together. Later Kusumoto told me that the maidservant who had discovered me collapsed on the veranda had left her husband in charge while she raced off to find the old couple out on their walk. It was not hard for them to understand the truth once they realized that Tsuyuko could not be found and that I, even though ill, had dressed and was about to go off. Suspecting what our plans were, they split up to search for Tsuyuko, who was discovered leaning against a post at the bus stop near the bridge by the foot of the mountain. Since Tsuyuko had probably not been able to offer any defense against her grandfather's very reasonable, very just probings of her intentions, she was, without further discussion, obliged to return with them to Tokyo. I, not to mention Kusumoto, had no idea what had happened to Tsuyuko after that, but the very thought that she had been confined under much stricter surveillance than before made me curse myself for my powerlessness.

"But tell me, how did you know I was here?"

"How?" Kusumoto laughed, an evasive look on his face. "A letter came from Yotsuya."

After receiving this letter he had gone to the Saijō house right away and a man who was obviously a servant had come out to tell him in detail about the events in Gōra, finally requesting that Kusumoto come to get me. My mind filled with shame as I imagined how shabbily Kusumoto must have been received at the Saijō house because of his connection to me, although he himself said nothing about that.

Once again I remained in my house and resumed my life of passing the days without saying a word to my wife. I didn't go out at all and as much as possible tried to keep Tsuyuko from my mind, but this proved impossible. My love for her was like a snake shut up in its hole during the winter months—it continued to throb with life but seemed dormant. Occasionally Kusumoto came over to visit, seemingly relieved to find me returned to my domestic routine. "You look as if you've settled down," he told me one day as he handed over a sealed letter from Tsuyuko. He said that when we were about to leave the Gōra estate, the maidservant had called him over for a private word and told him to give me the letter after I returned to Tokyo. Once alone, I quickly broke the seal. On the very morning of our trouble, Tsuyuko had stolen away from her grandparents and had written the letter in an obvious rush. The style, so rough and nervous that I could feel her anger rising up from her writing, showed the hard battle she had waged with her emotions. The harsh words also conveyed tremendous desperation and sadness:

> This is the end. Now it's good-bye. You'd better make the same decision for yourself too. Please decide! From today on, Tsuyuko does not belong to you anymore. Tsuyuko is Tsuyuko and you are you. You are alone. Please forgive me for writing such a cruel thing, but if I did not think this way I know exactly what would happen. I am a bad woman. If I were with you, your life would be completely destroyed. Do you understand this? You mustn't think about wanting us to be together. Now we are nothing. Nothing. From today on, even I will be able to forget all about you.

I was so stunned that my mind went blank, and I just singled out certain words without trying to comprehend what was written there.

> I am afraid for you. You say that you don't know what lengths you will go to next, but I know what a person like you will do.

66

You will gradually descend further and further into the pit. Even
though it isn't what I would want, I would be the one to send
you rushing to the bottom. I don't exactly know why it happens
but the more we think that we want to be together, the more
impossible it is for the two of us. We are digging our own holes.
Do you understand? That's what I'm afraid of. Do you know
what would happen next? We would both die. But I am not
afraid of dying. I'm afraid of what would happen before that.
You do understand, don't you? You see how it has gradually
become impossible? You see, don't you, Jōji? But don't think
that I am a coward. I must stop now and go no further. I am all
right. I am all right. I can say good-bye. Good-bye. I am going to
America on the *Tatsuta Maru,* on November 4th. It's good-bye
to everything. Please don't come searching for me anymore.

I read the letter again. Maybe because I had read it quickly I had misunderstood what she meant. Or perhaps there were hidden messages
that were not obvious at first. But I had misread nothing. My mind
tossed and turned in enormous distress as the events of that morning
came surging back. Tsuyuko had certainly waited for me at the bus
stop at the foot of the hill to make our escape. Could her feelings
have undergone such a complete change in the one or two hours
after her grandparents had found her and before her return to
Tokyo? And what had caused this transformation? Every answer I
could think of pierced me like a flight of arrows. Perhaps Tsuyuko
had never wanted to flee. After talking with me so often, perhaps
she simply couldn't see her way out of it and had gone against her
own inclinations in agreeing to my plans for escape. Was she now
breathing a sigh of relief at getting away from me? The disaster on
the day of the Kabuki had probably shown her how incompetent I
was in dealing with life. Had she agreed to flee on a whim, but then
soon lost interest?

I kept going over and over these possibilities but since I remained
unconvinced by each and every one of them, I thought that perhaps
she had been forced to write the letter under her grandparents' surveillance. And even if the letter correctly reflected her emotional
state, I couldn't bear it that she was left with those feelings. I won't
let you go to America, I whispered in my heart to Tsuyuko, whose
whereabouts were still a complete mystery to me. Then I remem-

bered hearing Tsuyuko talk about a cousin her mother had wanted her to marry, a man who worked for Mitsubishi in New York. Yet I found myself insisting that she was just lying, to distance herself from me, when she claimed she was going to America. Even so, with this one letter, Tsuyuko had succeeded in camouflaging her true state of mind. The very words she had written in the letter rang false. Was the Tsuyuko I knew a complete fabrication? I wanted to find out the truth, I wanted to see Tsuyuko and hear what she had to say for herself.

For the second time, just as I had done a month before, I became completely undone by my search for Tsuyuko. An objective observer would have concluded that I had taken leave of my senses, for I went to ask Oyae of the Yūyūtei in Shimbashi to call Tsuyuko's house and make up some lie about why she was calling. I would loiter about the front of Tsuyuko's house in Yotsuya until late at night, waiting for a car to return, and then question the driver about what was happening in the house. I simply lost control and let my days become consumed in useless activity. But since my search turned up nothing, it dawned on me that perhaps she really was going off to America and that she at least wanted to see me at the dock for a polite, distant good-bye. There was no other way to explain why she had informed me about her departure in her letter. Since this was my last hope, I had to wait for November 4th, the day the *Tatsuta Maru* would be sailing.

It was a clear, cold morning. I had called the ship office several times the week before, and took a train to the pier somewhat earlier than necessary. When I arrived at Yokohama the ship was waiting, having already completed preparations for departure. The pier and the deck teemed with people, but I made my way through the crowd and went up into the ship, finding no trace of Tsuyuko though I searched from the first class promenade to the middle deck, from the salon to the restaurant. When they talk about a person's eyes getting bloodshot from a desperate search, that was my state as I stood in the crowds wracked by the violence in my soul—no matter where Tsuyuko was hidden, I had to locate her. I found the ship's head purser and had him show me the list of passengers, but didn't see the name Saijō Tsuyuko anywhere.

"Do you have her request for a reservation?" I asked.

"No. We didn't receive a request," the head purser answered brusquely.

Soon the gong rang requesting that the visitors disembark. Jostled about within this scene of countless partings, I descended alone to the wharf. The departing ship's steam whistle sounded as if it were about to split the air in two. "Banzai!" "Sayonara!" Numerous cries mixed with the music coming from the ship as people tried to leave nothing unsaid in that brief final moment. To me it was apparent why the ship music was playing—every note cried out, "Hurry and find me!" I careened blindly through the streamers, thinking that even if Tsuyuko were hidden on board the ship, her mother and father or grandmother and grandfather or even that aunt I had seen at the Kabuki would surely be among the crowd to see her off. This became my firm conviction, but perhaps because I could hardly see straight from distress, I didn't find them. The ship pulled away from the shore so slowly that it seemed not to be moving at all. Numerous streamers fluttered from the ship's deck and in another moment the people there faded into the distance. For a long while I stood and stared at the ship. Had Tsuyuko boarded under an assumed name to avoid me? It would have been easy for one young woman to hide among the throngs on that huge ship. Extremely depressed, I walked along the pier where the crowds had already thinned out. By then I was past being assailed by the intense emotions that had gripped me when I read Tsuyuko's letter. Whatever happens will happen, I whispered, tears pouring down my cheeks as I commiserated with myself over my own hapless inability to battle the world.

After that I remained secluded in my house. Whenever the thought of Tsuyuko came floating into my mind, I don't know why but I was convinced she was still in Japan. I simply sensed she was still in the country, though I couldn't say where. Perhaps this was just a straw I was clutching to improve my spirits, but at last I decided to go out and look for her. One day I was on a street corner in Surugadai going toward Meiji University when I saw a girl with her hair hanging loose who looked exactly like Tsuyuko from the back. I was so surprised I ran after her, about to call out. She must have heard my footsteps, though, for she stopped and looked back.

No wonder I'd thought she was Tsuyuko—she was the girl who'd been playing the piano in the room facing the Yotsuya house's back garden. Her narrow shoulders and the play of shadows around her eyes were definitely just like Tsuyuko's, but on her pale lips I saw a slightly childish and haughty smile. Perhaps it was only my state of mind at the time, but the smile also seemed to speak of deep understanding and compassion. As I stared at her, I could hear the Chopin melody she had played each night. My disappointment was soon jumbled with a kind of happiness—I had at least been able to find a relative of Tsuyuko's on this street corner.

"Just a moment," I called out to her. "Excuse me, but aren't you Saijō-san?" She silently looked at my face and since her eyes told me that she knew who I was, I boldly asked her about Tsuyuko. "She never left, did she?"

"No, you're wrong, she left," she answered clearly. "She left on the *Tatsuta Maru*."

"*Tatsuta Maru?* But I even went to the ship to look for her."

A shrewd, adult expression came to the girl's eyes. "My sister left from Kobe." Then she turned at the corner coffee shop and walked off.

I was stunned. What could this mean? Did Tsuyuko leave from Kobe because she was afraid I would pursue her? I felt like crumbling right there on that windy street. Was Tsuyuko that afraid of me? Did she want to get away from me that much? And now was I to believe that Tsuyuko, who just that morning I'd felt sure was still somewhere in Japan—had that same Tsuyuko already arrived in America, been welcomed by her cousin, and at that very moment was cozily riding with him on the train to New York? Beyond this confusion, I was also painfully aware of the contempt and disgust Tsuyuko's family felt toward me. As my anguish grew, controlling it was out of the question. Of course, I didn't want to let the matter rest, but frankly what choice did I have? Only one recourse remained: I would most likely fritter away the strength that still remained in me, the strength I had been drawing on to keep up the memory of the Tsuyuko I had lost.

· · ·

In no time the story of my failed romance became a subject of gossip among my friends. Kusumoto sometimes drolly informed me that there was one faction which contended that I might kill myself and another insisting I was not the type to lose myself over some love affair. In Kusumoto's drollness there was obviously a great feeling of friendship for me. "It's just a bad joke for a man to fall in love, don't you agree?" he would remark, talking in that vein to get me to think of my shattered romance as just a minor amusement. Occasionally, almost inadvertently, I found myself being persuaded by Kusumoto's words, or perhaps it was a conscious decision on my part to try and be persuaded. Of course he's right, I'm not capable of losing myself over a love affair, am I?

I tried this line of thought, going back to the time eight years before when I had got together with my wife, or the women I had lived with abroad—those affairs had hardly been cases of love. Had I ever once been in love? Never. That was because I wasn't the type of man who falls in love, was I? I had in fact become nothing more than a scoundrel who had cleverly learned his lessons while abroad. It was just that now my expertise had developed further and I was able to put on a show of falling in love. Would such a person fall seriously in love only where Tsuyuko was concerned, and then have his heart broken? It was utterly ridiculous of my friends to say that I might kill myself over this. When I was able to keep myself on this track I could see the suffocating end of my relations with Tsuyuko in its comic light. Somehow it was pleasant to think that I had never been in love with her, but had merely been roped in by her peculiar talent for running away and then beckoning me to come to her from that distance. After all, wasn't it merely natural that the kind of scoundrel I'd become would respond to the challenge of snaring such an overprotected young girl? I had been smothered by intense emotions for so long, but at last I felt some relief as my feelings for Tsuyuko went under review. "It's only over a woman," I would say to myself, and in the process became convinced that at least from that day forward I would become the person I used to be. I went out on the town, danced, drank, and amused myself with women. I thought I might actually become what I had been before—a man who only thought of women as interesting playthings. This attitude came easily—people whose hearts were broken, who no longer cared what happened to them, assumed the same pose. But it wasn't that I was drinking because I had no concern for the consequences; rather, I'd begun to doubt whether life had any purpose at all.

Although I kept up my resolve to return to my old habits, when I went out on the streets carousing with my friends I found it an effort to keep myself entertained. One day I suddenly thought, what if I went to America? I had heard much about wandering Japanese who were called "American Japs." It might be amusing to live like that, going from one town to the next without any goal in life. That thought led me to toy with the bizarre idea that one day I might bump into Tsuyuko, quite by accident, on some city street corner. Then, as if parched by thirst, I found myself rummaging around for my old suitcase, looking up the ship timetables, and the total cost of the trip. But my mind had not become so addled that I overlooked my inability to find even a sen of the money for the fare or other expenses. How genuine was my desire to go to America? First of all, wasn't a trip to America simply out of the question because of the distance? I had to laugh at these impossible plans of mine. Then it occurred to me that if only something exciting were to burst upon me, I would let myself be enthralled and then my whole life would become more stable. I mulled over possible ways to save myself and increasingly went out on the town to have a look at what was waiting there for me.

One morning in the middle of winter, around Christmas, a telegram came from my friend Baba, saying that an amusing gathering was in progress and I should come over. Although Baba had been a friend since my days abroad, he was less a professional acquaintance than a person to be with when I was in the mood to have a good time. He had a fancy studio in Ushigome in Takadai and lived with his wife, a woman known for her beauty, but since this couple led a free, extremely modern kind of life, there was always some kind of uproar underway in their house. Throughout the day people who found this sort of thing interesting gathered there, as well as people who enjoyed having a good time. Since the telegram had come from Baba, I assumed that he had invited over a woman who would be memorable, and was planning to coddle me like a sick patient he was cheering up—or so I thought as I went over.

Even outside, as I tapped on the glass with my cane, I could hear the phonograph and the shrill laughter of young women. "Come on in," Baba yelled from inside. When I opened the door I saw three young women, each with her own special style—one, dressed like a traditional Japanese girl, wore her hair in an old-fashioned upsweep, another was vehemently flashy in a dance hall woman's kimono and bobbed hair, and the third had on a dress as sober as a mission school student's. Baba's friend Tsumura was talking with them.

"These young ladies are all your fans," he said. "They've been asking to be introduced to you for three months." Tsumura laughed and his special brand of sarcasm surfaced in his eyes, which narrowed like threads. Tsumura, the son of the owner of the Shinjuku bookstore Tsunokuniya, is now trying his hand at publishing magazines on literature and the arts, aside from managing Tsunokuniya. During that period he was still a bachelor and for a short while after holding an exhibit of works by Baba and myself upstairs at Tsunokuniya, he had shepherded us around just to amuse himself.

"Not three months. It's half a year." The woman with the bobbed hair interrupted him.

The women's cheeks were glowing from the warmth of the stove and the tea, which was spiked with whiskey. While we talked and danced, only the one woman who was dressed like a student sat with her legs stretched out on the floor as she gazed at the commotion we were making.

"Do you mind if I borrow this?" I asked, taking the mandolin she was holding.

I strummed along with the jazz recording, but no sooner had I started than Baba turned around and yelled at me. "Hey, stop showing off and trying to get all the women to fall for you!"

"What are you talking about?"

I returned the instrument to the woman and casually glanced at her legs peeping out from beneath her skirt, which, in the fashion of those days, only came down to her knees. For a Japanese woman she had unusually pretty, slender legs. When I looked up the woman also stole a glance at me with laughing eyes. I heard later that this woman had been having problems with her lungs for a long time and that explained why her features—with the particular characteristic of her illness—were soft, as if gently swollen. She was not exactly a beauty but had a sweet, womanly feeling, a strangely sensual air about her. Although she did not wear glasses, her nearsightedness was apparent in the way she would narrow her large eyes like a cat even to look at something close. I was not at all drawn to the other two women, but somehow this one caught my fancy. At that time I was urging myself to feel such emotions and so I don't know how much of my interest was genuine. In any case, that day we had an interesting time until dusk and then parted.

Three or four days later I had some business with Tsumura and as I was cutting across the plaza in front of Shinjuku Station I noticed the same woman at the bus stop. When I stopped to greet her, she did not seem aware of my presence although she was facing me directly. Is she that nearsighted, I wondered, when a tall student wearing a Keiō University uniform got out of the bus and went over to her. They spoke loudly as they passed with their arms entwined. After my business with Tsumura was finished, I told him my news. "I just saw that woman from the other night with her boyfriend."

"Is that so?" Tsumura laughed, narrowing his eyes. "But that Tomoko has been telling everyone that she's pining away for you."

"She's probably just saying that for effect, but somehow, to tell you the truth, that kind of woman does appeal to me."

We joked like that and then I returned home. But three or four days later while shopping in a Ginza department store I again ran into Tomoko, the woman in the Western-style dress, at the next counter. She was eagerly picking through neckties just five feet away but did not notice me. She had selected an appallingly flashy tie with a red plaid design and was having it wrapped when I tapped her on the shoulder.

"Well . . ." Tomoko immediately widened those half-closed, catlike eyes of hers.

"Did you buy that red necktie for a special friend of yours?"

"What a thing to say, Yuasa-san. I bought it for my brother." She told me that this brother was a great admirer of my paintings and wouldn't I come for a visit to her house one day. "Is tomorrow all right for you? Tomorrow is Sunday. Please come tomorrow. My brother will be there." I asked her the address of her home in Senzoku and promised to go there the next day.

Although the end of the year was fast approaching, for a person in my circumstances it was just another winter afternoon. The next day I was putting on my shoes before going out when my wife, who usually didn't come to the door to see me off, called out from behind.

"Have you signed that agreement yet?"

"I'm not signing it," I answered, without turning around.

The agreement was the contract concerning the money I would pay to my wife for food and education for our child, among other things. Once we had decided to divorce, each of us had written out our own terms on several occasions but no matter how often we did that, we couldn't come up with an agreement that both found acceptable. My wife had consulted with a lawyer friend and the new agreement had me paying one hundred yen each month for the child until he became an adult.

"Does this mean you won't agree to it at all?" she asked.

"Just think about it. One hundred yen. In the current state of my finances, how can you expect me to pay that kind of money every month?"

"If you can't, that's fine with me." She said nothing more.

My wife's state of mind was easy to understand. She had taken care of the child and waited for me to come home for a full seven years, but felt that if she had known I'd ask for a divorce as soon as I got back, she would certainly have spent those seven years differently. And, she thought, because of her irrevocably wasted seven years, wasn't I obliged to go along with the agreement even if it was beyond my means?

"No point arguing," I told her. "I don't see any sense in getting me to agree to something that I can't possibly fulfill."

If she agreed to fifty yen, I thought, then I might be able to work something out. And since we both wanted the divorce as quickly as possible, it seemed stupid to be thwarted by financial details, but what could we do about it? Lawyers, lawsuits, agreements—my wife's favorite words amused me as I walked through town. By the time I reached the railway station, however, my mind had turned to other matters.

Tomoko's house was close to the Senzoku Station in a quiet section of a newly constructed residential district. The houses in the area looked American, but the shrubbery on both sides of the narrow stone paths leading to the front doors and the gardens, which I could see in the back, were vaguely Japanese. The lack of harmony in the styles gave the area a modern air and her house, with a Chinese lantern hanging from the porch, suited the neighborhood. When I announced myself Tomoko came running out like a little girl, wearing that short skirt which came down to her knees. "Mother, Yuasa-san is here. Please come out!" There was a note of urgency in her voice and no sooner had she spoken than a woman who must have been Tomoko's mother came following out after her. She was decidedly overweight and looked about forty. "Welcome." She spoke with gentle charm as she led me into the parlor. There was an old-fashioned chandelier and a Chinese picture scroll hung on the wall. The jumble of flowers as well as the other knicknacks on the mantelpiece and the table gave the house a warmly intimate, lived-in feeling. I felt strangely at ease as I sat down.

"I see that Tomoko has once again been thinking only of herself and imposed on you—" the mother began.

"Mama said that you wouldn't come."

"How can you say that?" the mother interrupted. "Now who would want to have anything to do with a naughty girl like you? Why don't you tell Yoshi to bring in a load of firewood?"

"No, I don't want to. You go. And also bring us something good to eat."

"What am I going to do with you?" The mother laughed as she stood up and went out.

"You have a nice mother," I said, feeling envious of the very natural affections between mother and daughter. This is what a home is supposed to be like, I thought, remembering that after I had returned to Japan from my long stay abroad and tried to settle down, my house had become just another of my temporary residences. On my frequent visits to Tomoko's afterwards, I was constantly gripped by the feeling that while I'd destroyed my own chances for a home, I, homeless as I was, had found in their house a precious commodity that I'd lost in my youth.

"My mother won't come back."

"You understand everything about your mother?"

"My mother understands me."

"Every naughty thing you do?"

"Yes." Then Tomoko added quietly, "It's because I'm sick."

"I know that," I answered evenly.

Tomoko got up to put more wood on the fire, but I offered to do it instead and as I added on the log, I glanced at her face, saying, "The sickness gives your face its charm. You're pale even when you stand by the fire."

"Do you like pale faces?"

"Yes, I do."

With her blurred, swollen features, Tomoko looked as if she had emerged from a black and white photograph. Even her lips were pale. If drawn skillfully, her portrait would have been interesting. Then too, after talking with her for a while, I discovered in her voice, in her expressions and the way she spoke, the same "fascination with the colorless" revealed in her face.

"My sister puts on airs, you know." Her younger brother stuck his head in and made Tomoko laugh with his teasing.

Shortly after, I took my leave. The mother had not, as Tomoko predicted, reappeared in the room but now she came hurrying forward and repeatedly urged me to stay longer because her husband would be coming home soon. I made my excuses and went out to the front garden. Tomoko, who had rushed out of the house ahead of me, stood near the shrubs with a shawl as big as a blanket over her shoulders.

"Shall I go to the station with you?"

"You look like a Spanish woman in that shawl. Aren't you cold with just that on?"

Although she shook her head slightly, she did seem to feel the cold for she stuck close to me, trying to hide from the chill. No wind blew, but there was a pond nearby and the coolness of the suburban dusk swept over my skin. While we walked I put my arm gently around Tomoko.

"You're cold, aren't you?"

"Yes."

In the dim light I was moved by Tomoko's expression, which had blurred even further, bringing to her face the pliancy of a woman who would readily submit to a man. Her body felt as light as a feather beneath her shawl when I stopped to embrace and kiss her.

"Please—again." Tomoko whispered so softly that I could barely hear her.

Once more I embraced and kissed her. A lingering sense of the warm fireplace and the cozy atmosphere in her house had lodged in my heart: holding Tomoko in my arms was a continuation of that pleasure.

"Now go home." I spoke to her as if she were a baby. "You'll catch a cold."

"When will I see you again?"

"Any time you want." And after agreeing to meet her the next day, I got on the train.

Suddenly very cheerful, I left my house the next afternoon and the next to visit Tomoko. Perhaps it isn't absolutely correct to say I went to visit Tomoko, for I was stirred more by the desire to wrap myself in a chair in that comfortable house. Nor was it Tomoko's gentle eyes and face that welled up in my heart first, but rather her mother's affectionate voice, the warm coffee, the bright flickering light. When I sat down before the fire in that house, I felt at peace, as if I had finally come home from a long journey. After the intense pressure of my love for Tsuyuko, my relationship with a woman like Tomoko was so serene that the word "love" didn't even occur to me. Perhaps for that reason alone I liked Tomoko.

I gradually became on good terms with her family too, and even Tomoko's father, who at first had viewed my visits to his young daughter with extreme vigilance, began to treat me like an intimate friend. Sometimes I visited the house and talked only with him. Since he had lived in America for a long time, he had adopted completely American habits and behaved more like a good friend to his children than a father. He let his children do whatever they wanted and always thought of their wishes first before proceeding. "That's because," he would always explain, "they really didn't think I was going to live." The severe pulmonary tuberculosis he had suffered from in his youth had been miraculously cured following a spiritual crisis. Since his life, which seemed fated to last only up to that time, had been spared by this miracle, he considered the rest of his days a complete "windfall." To make best use of his windfall, he often said, he had resolved to help other people as much as possible, and in his cheerful, good-natured way he would distribute to his workers a booklet he had written about how to lead a good life. Deep gratitude was all I could feel for the sunny atmosphere of the house where this father lived—I shuddered to recall how I had been so coldly received at Tsuyuko's home, where they had treated me as if I were nothing but a beggar. Once the New Year passed, I went to Tsumura's office after a long absence.

"Is it true what I hear, that you're going to marry Tomoko?" Tsumura asked me right away.

"Where did you hear that nonsense?"

"That's what people are saying. The rumor is that Tomoko is completely taken with the idea, even though you might not be so inclined." He grinned as usual while his narrowed eyes showed a trace of criticism. "There will be trouble later, I'm telling you."

"There won't be any trouble since I can't get married—actually, I just don't know how to go about settling things with my wife."

"But Tomoko doesn't know anything about your family troubles, does she?"

"Of course she knows and her mother probably does too."

That was my response to Tsumura's scrutiny but I wasn't telling the whole truth. From the start, Tomoko had known about my wife and child and also about Tsuyuko. When I talked about Tsuyuko, she had joked, "Why don't we go to America together to find her?" But she didn't seem at all concerned about my wife, perhaps because I had spoken of that relationship as a matter more easily dismissed than was actually the case. I had never dreamed of marrying Tomoko, but if she now showed some interest in that direction, one would have difficulty denying that I had at least hinted that it actually would be easy for us to marry. At that time I hadn't analyzed my own thoughts deeply and believed that even if the trouble Tsumura had predicted were to occur, it would all work out somehow.

"Don't worry. I won't make such a blunder," I assured him.

"Remember, a young woman can be a lot of trouble even if she behaves as if she's very naughty and experienced. If things get sticky, you'll make an utter fool of yourself. And, most of all, don't forget that while I personally don't care about you divorcing your wife, your older colleagues will disapprove."

Tsumura urged me to return to my own family since he believed that keeping my home together, for form's sake alone, was wisest, no matter how I really felt about living there. In this he echoed the opinions of those who put great stock in public opinion. Hadn't my wife waited for her husband's return for such a long time? While I had heard these criticisms, they no longer concerned me in the least. Still I didn't want any trouble over Tomoko and so for an extended period I gave up going to her house. At the same time, though totally unrelated to this, I wanted to settle the divorce proceedings with my wife as quickly as possible. I maintained that we could always take care of the last details at our convenience afterwards. My wife agreed that we should file the divorce notification and so I wrote it out and my wife also signed. Someone from my wife's side had to serve as a guarantor, but the designated person had apparently refused, saying, "I don't know why, but signing a divorce agreement would weigh on my conscience."

When I heard this, a most unpleasant expression came to my face. "If he feels that way, why didn't he refuse to be a guarantor from the beginning?"

"I'll go to Shibayama's place. He'll understand." My wife went out but quickly returned to inform me that her friend Shibayama was off on a trip and wouldn't come back for a few days.

Although I had the feeling that my wife was trying to delay the process, since only the signature of her guarantor was missing, I did feel somewhat relieved at the steps we had taken and for the first time in a long while sketched the view from my second story window. Then I heard my wife coming up from below.

"Tell me," my wife smiled, "even if we get divorced, we'll still treat each other like relatives, won't we? I mean, if I have some problem, is it all right if I come to talk to you about it?"

"That would be fine." What nerve she had! Every once in a while such pretty sentences would pass mildly from my wife's lips as if she had made a discovery. But I knew perfectly well that my wife would go ahead and do the exact opposite of what she said, since any number of times this habit of hers had caused me no small displeasure.

I had stayed in my house for ten days, entertaining bleak thoughts, when Baba surprised me one afternoon by paying a visit.

"Something terrible has happened. Tomoko has swallowed some sleeping pills."

Tomoko's friend Momoko, the woman with the bobbed hair and flashy kimono, had gone to Baba's house with this news, instructing him to tell me to go to Tomoko's house immediately. She couldn't have done such a stupid thing, I reassured myself in something of a panic. She didn't try to kill herself with those sleeping pills. She told me that she'd had a lot of trouble sleeping. Saying this did little to erase the great distress I felt as I made preparations to leave, still unable to believe that Tomoko had attempted suicide. When I arrived at her house I couldn't decide whether it seemed quieter than usual.

"Where is the young lady?"

"She's resting in her room," came the reply.

The mother always came out to the front hall but when she did not appear I attributed it to a change in the whole atmosphere during my absence. Tomoko was lying on the bed, her face pale.

"What happened? Did you get worse again?"

It might have been that the curtains were closed in the middle of the day, making the room dark, but when Tomoko opened her eyes and nodded in agreement, her large eyes loomed like two black holes. The shadows on her soft, vaguely contoured cheeks made her look drawn and exhausted.

"You didn't come to see me for a long time."

"Me?" I feigned ignorance but found that I wanted to please her. "I was working. I drew a picture of you."

"Did you?" She smiled. While the reports of a suicide attempt may have been false, I felt her sadness must have been my fault in some way and I wanted to be as kind to her as possible.

Her mother soon entered and when Tomoko wasn't looking she beckoned me out of the room. "Are you busy tonight?"

"What happened? Has something happened to Tomoko?"

"There's been some trouble. She's had a slight hemorrhage. If you're not busy, I do have something I'd like to discuss with you tonight." She took a black fur wrap from the maid and placed it over her shoulders. "I have to go out now, but do you know the Chinese restaurant Aoba? Behind Shōwa Avenue? Could you meet me there around six o'clock?"

I was startled for I saw no reason why we had to go elsewhere to talk, but of course those questions could wait until we met and so I agreed to her request. She went to the front door, only to come back again and say, "Please don't say anything to Tomoko about this. I don't want her to worry." After the mother had gone out, I visited with Tomoko long enough to be convinced that her weak, pathetic appearance was, as her mother had explained, a debilitation resulting from the hemorrhage. The story about the sleeping pills was just a meddlesome melodrama that Momoko had invented. I felt much relieved when I went to the Aoba Restaurant near Shōwa Avenue at the appointed time.

Tomoko's mother was already waiting for me. "Will you have a drink? Some Lao-chiu perhaps?" She continued to chatter even after the food was brought in, and only after some time paused in her talk to ask me casually, "Tell me, will matters with your wife be settled soon?"

I spoke to her honestly of the recent developments, but vaguely surmising her motives, didn't mention our intractable money problems. "I'd like to move if I could find a suitable place," I said in summary, unable to suppress a slight fear.

Just as I'd anticipated, the mother wanted to discuss Tomoko. "My husband says that since she's sick, we can't expect her to marry in the usual manner. He thinks we should have her take a course in English on accounting and if she wants to, have her work at our own company and eventually become a businesswoman who doesn't have to do too much. But I don't entirely agree with him. I keep thinking that even though she's ill there are many people with her illness who marry. And no one can be sure that she'll never recover. Look at my husband, he was sick like that and he's as strong as an ox now."

I drank my liquor silently, gradually becoming so dumbfounded by the implications of the mother's words that I suspected I might soon be incapable of moving. But I still had time to arrange my thoughts as she continued: "Don't you agree with me? If she could move to a new environment, maybe her health would improve. Even if she became worse again . . ." She closed her mouth slightly. "If she gets so bad that she dies, that makes me even more determined to do whatever she wants. Maybe I'm just a foolish parent, but that child may die soon. Two or three months, at the most half a year, I think. During that time, I want her to be happy. You know all about her illness, Yuasa-san, and it's only for two or three months. Do you think you could live with her? You wouldn't find that objectionable, would you?" She gazed at me and in her gentle eyes I saw a glittering light, but when tears hid the light I became flustered and looked away.

Although I should have had an answer prepared, those unexpected tears confused my thinking. "Is Tomoko that bad?"

"I really don't know." She smiled in her sincere way. "But since she is so unpredictable, don't you think that she just might improve? That's why I'm asking you to help us. You're only worried about your wife, isn't that true? Once you get your affairs settled with your wife, you will marry Tomoko, won't you?"

"Right now, I can't do anything about your suggestion. It's not as if I've already separated from my wife."

"But it is only a matter of time, isn't it?"

"Yes, of course." I was unwilling to say anything further. Tsumura had warned me that there would be trouble later, and that moment had finally come. Since I couldn't reveal my true feelings, Tomoko's mother stared at me as I sat there silently. In a moment, however, her mood brightened.

"Think this over carefully. And please don't tell Tomoko or anyone else what we have discussed this evening." She lifted a plump wrist and checked the time. "The doctor will be coming and so you'll have to excuse me. You will come and see us again in a few days?"

"Of course."

We took the same taxi to the Kamata Station on the Keihin Line, where we parted. When I was alone I realized that far from rejecting the mother's proposal, I had anticipated that day for some time, actually had been waiting for it. No shuddering fear wracked my body when I let myself think, "So it looks as if I am going to marry Tomoko after all."

My wife was in the tea room knitting a jacket for our child when I got home. I had just put my shoes into the shoe holder and was going up to the second floor when I turned around to ask, "Has Shibayama come back?"

"Not yet." She answered coldly, without looking at me. "But I've decided to take care of that after the other agreements have been completed."

"What do you mean?"

"The proper order is to see to that matter only after the other agreements are settled. And Shibayama will be coming home soon."

"But since we're going to get a divorce anyway, I think you should start looking for a house. If you don't want to move, then I'll leave."

My wife remained silent, but the next day she returned home late at night and came tapping up to the second floor. I could tell that she had an announcement to make, for she smiled brightly as she tried to get my attention: "Tell me, how much do you really think you'll be able to pay me every month?"

"One hundred yen is out of the question."

Some change was taking place in my wife's state of mind and I could see that she was lost in her own thoughts, becoming somewhat sullen. "Tell me, how much do you feel you'd be comfortable paying me?"

"Fifty yen. If we make it fifty yen, I could probably raise the money somehow."

My wife mused upon this and at last declared that fifty yen would be fine. Fifty yen would only pay for the rent and be enough to make ends meet, but upon reflection she had decided that it was unbearable to go on living as if we were forever in a state of siege, with me upstairs and her downstairs. She also feared that the child's personality would become warped. "Now I plan to start all over again," she announced. "I'm going to take lessons in Western tailoring and open up a shop with a friend. Tomorrow I'll find a small house." She then made a lively descent down the stairs. Whoever she had met that day must have provided her with this wisdom. It amused me to think that she was only arranging matters as I had wished.

. . .

One afternoon a few days later, I went to Tomoko's house and was surprised to find her father working in the front garden. He stood up to greet me, throwing aside the trowel he had in his hand and quickly inviting me to come in through the veranda. I always went to the parlor but this time he led me to his private room.

"I heard that Yasuko spoke to you. I want you to know that it would really be a great service to us if you would marry Tomoko, since you know all about her illness. Actually I had pretty much given up finding someone for her."

"Has Tomoko recovered?"

"If you hadn't come today, I thought I'd go to see you myself. Then that sickness of hers would have vanished pretty quickly. If we're going to do something good, then it's best to be quick about it, don't you think? We'll only invite our closest friends and relatives and have the bare minimum for a wedding. Just a moment—" He called out to a room beyond, "Will someone get the calendar from the second floor study?"

Tomoko's mother must have reported our conversation as if I'd already agreed to the marriage. Actually, I wasn't surprised when I heard the father talk in that vein, for my ambiguous attitude must have convinced Tomoko's parents that we would marry. In fact, I had already toyed with the idea of becoming a member of that warm, genial family. In the end, didn't it all amount to the same thing? I would cut my festering relations with my wife, build a new life with Tomoko, and from time to time her parents would visit us. It caused me no discomfort to think that this might come to pass.

The father looked through the calendar the maid brought in, muttering phrases I couldn't always catch about this day or that being inauspicious. Since he was in a rush to set the wedding date, his calculations started out fourteen or fifteen days away and gradually came closer.

"Let's make it the 23rd. It may be a little too soon and we'll be rushing around. But the 23rd is the best day."

With only five days remaining until the 23rd, I was absolutely confounded by this pronouncement. My worries were in no small way related to the whole question of whether my affairs could be settled by then, but the father's impatient manner easily overpowered my own objections.

"I don't think it's necessary to have a formal ceremony," I managed to say.

"We'll just do it as perfunctorily as possible. I'll have to, for the people at the company."

In a moment the mother came in and decisions quickly followed regarding what hall to use for the ceremony and who should act as the go-between. It occurred to me that I had, in a matter of minutes, become the bridegroom of that family.

"Yuasa-san, can I speak to you a moment?" The mother called me over later with worry in her voice. "Has your wife decided where she's going to live?"

"I think she went looking for a place this morning."

"Is that so? I'm happy to hear that." She spoke with such evident relief that I couldn't help repeating that she had no reason to worry about my wife. From then on, it seemed to me, I'd have to do everything required to marry Tomoko, even if my domestic situation became more complicated.

No wonder that I felt rushed and arrived home while it was still daylight. My wife was standing at the entrance, evidently on the lookout for my return.

"I found a very good house. Six mats, plus four and a half plus three. The rent is thirteen yen."

"Did you agree to take it?"

"Well, I want you to go and look at it with me. If you like it, then I'll move tomorrow morning."

This splendid turn of events made me secretly rejoice as I went with my wife to look at the house. The place was close to the railroad tracks but there were plums and other trees in the garden. The house was a separate establishment with its own gate in front, rather old, but not at all uncomfortable.

"Looks all right to me," I told her.

"It's good, isn't it? The rent is thirteen yen, which I think is too much, but once I move in I'll get them to reduce it to twelve." Her spirits high, my wife didn't have the slightest suspicion about what was in my heart.

Early the next morning when I heard the clattering noises of their packing, I got up and helped them move. After we mended the paper on the sliding doors and put the chests of drawers and brazier in place, the place did start to look cozy.

"Oh, I am so happy." My wife laughed, genuinely pleased. "Be sure to send us that fifty yen every month. Really, I don't see why I didn't move sooner. When we were living together you didn't even give me pocket money."

I returned to our old home alone. The other houses in the neighborhood had their lights on, but ours stood in complete darkness. With all our possessions moved out, the interior of the house welcomed me with the coldness of a dark cave. I went up to the second floor and threw myself down amidst my remaining easels and canvases. For a long time I slept, my mind racing even in its dreams. At last I was alone, but this state of affairs afforded me not an iota of pleasure.

The next day I carried out a few of my paintings and went to visit a patron of mine who owned a bookstore in Kōjimachi. I felt relaxed enough to be able to talk about my wedding plans, and this change in my circumstances pleased him, since he'd been disturbed about the utter futility of my attachment to Tsuyuko. Without saying a word he gave me five hundred yen. Once I had that money I immediately went looking for a place to live, since the prospect of spending another day in that cold cave of a house did not please me in the slightest. I searched through the residential section of Ōmori and soon found a suitable Western-style house which a foreign couple had just vacated. Then I went right over to Tomoko's house in Senzoku to discuss this.

"Well, that's good news," the mother said. "Since my husband is so casual about these things, I was concerned. I'd like to go over and see the house." As she was putting on her coat, Tomoko suddenly announced that she wanted to go with us.

"You can't go," the mother protested. "You'll get worse, and only cause more problems."

"I'll be all right. Jōji, as long as I don't get caught in the wind, I'll be all right." Tomoko had only recently become well enough to get out of bed and her breath was rough as she went ahead to the car.

"It's not such a great house," I said as I wrapped the blanket around Tomoko's thin legs.

"I don't care what kind of house it is. I'll wear those wooden shoes of mine in the house. What do you think, Mama?" Tomoko spoke happily, like a schoolgirl going on a field trip. The wooden shoes were apparently a present she'd received from someone who'd been abroad.

The trip from Senzoku to that house in Ōmori took less than seven minutes by taxi. In the distance we could see the house's pointed red roof surrounded by a grove of old trees, and the sunny second floor window with its white iron shutters.

"My, what a nice house," the mother exclaimed, smiling and turning toward Tomoko. "There are those roses you like in the hedge."

They liked the place more than I expected and enthusiastically went around looking at each room. Discussions ensued about putting the piano near this window, or whether the dog could be tied up on the veranda.

"It really is quite sunny, isn't it?" I whispered this to the mother in the solicitous tones I'd taken up as part of my new role.

The next day I transported my paintings and other possessions from the house in Kamata. With all the household goods passed along to my wife, I had to arrange to buy everything I needed and that task took up one whole day of searching in second-hand shops specializing in Western-style household goods. I bought a sofa and display shelves, then put up some curtains. They had already sent over Tomoko's cheery, very feminine household items from Senzoku. Two days before the wedding, I sent out simple invitations to the few friends who were aware of my situation. It was likely that not a single one of them would attend the wedding. As I was writing the addresses of A and B and C as well as Kusumoto and Baba and Tsumura, I could picture their faces. "A wedding? Tell me, who is he going to marry now?" "What is this? Second marriage, third marriage, it's all the same to him. There's going to be some interesting developments after this, I'm sure." "People are just not going to let him get away with this kind of immorality, divorcing his wife and all." I knew all about their opinions, but what did I care? No matter how much they may have objected, I couldn't go on living as before and thus I prepared myself to be able to sit there unconcerned even if no one showed up at the wedding. Finally the day arrived. I got ready and before going over to the Josuikan in Shiba for the ceremony, I stopped off at Tomoko's house.

"Welcome!" The mother was of course unable to hide the happiness on her face. "We've been extremely busy. There's so much confusion you'd think we were at war."

Many of Tomoko's girlfriends from school had come carrying bouquets and dressed in absolute splendor. The members of the household rushed about among these guests on various chores and at times even seemed to have forgotten that I was there. The cars to transport the people to the ceremony had already arrived in front.

"What's happened to Tomoko?" I asked.

"Tomoko? Tomoko? Now really, where is she?"

I put on my shoes ahead of the others and stood by myself in the entranceway but I didn't see Tomoko anywhere. Then I took a casual walk around the shrubs in front and made my way toward a side door where, through an opening in the window curtains, I saw Tomoko standing inside with a tall young boy in a Keiō University uniform, apparently having a secret talk. Amazed, I hid myself behind some bushes. I remembered that once, when I had first known Tomoko, I had come upon her beside a bus stop in front of Shinjuku Station and she had walked right past me, her arm entwined with this same Keiō student's. Tomoko, wearing a radiant pale peach wedding dress and still carrying her big bouquet, had her handkerchief at her eye. She was crying. "Now what is this all about?" I wondered.

And then I decided I would simply behave like that urbane husband I had seen in American films—the kind who makes cynical jokes about the goings on in his own household. Just like that urbane husband, I'd pretend not to have seen anything of my wife's romance. In this way, of course, my superiority would be indisputable. But when I quietly moved away from the window and hid in the car, calm was hardly my principal emotion. She was crying. That woman who had wanted to marry me, who had supposedly even taken sleeping pills—that woman was crying. All the pleasure drained out of me. I smoked a cigarette and began to consider the matter. From the outset, I conceded, I had remained far removed from any bright rays of hope or pleasurable twinges of expectation—sensations that would have been expected of someone who hoped to get a new start in life by marrying Tomoko. No great love for Tomoko had spurred me into this, but rather my heart had been drawn to the warm atmosphere of her home and only for that reason did I want to make such a change in my life. Just as I was concluding that the urbane husband was actually the most astute role to adopt, Tomoko came out, assisted by her mother.

"What are we to do—she's behaving just like a baby." The mother spoke brightly. "Why, she may be getting married but she says she's heartbroken about leaving this house. Look at her. Her eyes are all red."

Of course I was well aware that this was not what Tomoko had on her mind. At the hall, many people had arrived, for despite their promise to invite only five or six of their closest friends, forty or fifty people were already gathered there. The guests were either Tomoko's relatives or from her father's company—not a single one of my friends had come.

After introducing me to each guest, the father kept asking me quietly, "What happened? I don't see anyone from your side."

"All my friends are rather casual about these things. You can understand—they think weddings are rather foolish." It was clear to me that no one would come, but even then the father seemed to think this was impossible.

"Shall we wait for a bit?" the mother also inquired.

Tomoko, her eyes red and swollen from her tears, was surrounded by many of her friends and she occasionally stole a look at me. The three of them kept silent, but their disappointment was obvious.

Even though I'd said that no one would come, they still seemed to expect that soon some car would stop outside and a crowd of my friends would come barging in, and that newspaper photographers, having caught wind of the story, would arrive and fill the whole room with the popping of their flashbulbs. That was their hope, but I of course hadn't wished to broadcast my news to my relatives, or to the newspapers, the magazines, or even to my friends. What people would say about what I was doing did generate some anxiety in me. Apparently, the speeches about discarding or not discarding my wife and child—from the script of that long drawn-out and foolish drama—had seeped into my brain. From the very beginning, I hadn't wanted to invite anyone. I'd decided that as a first step I would just marry Tomoko and after that, gradually step out into society. But then I saw what an odd situation I'd created for myself, since there was not a single person there from the groom's side. Had anyone ever seen such a marriage ceremony? Would this be marked as the first strange, shaky episode in the life I was to begin with Tomoko? I secretly sorted through these issues while trying to put on an appearance of calm.

"Well, it was, I admit, arranged rather hastily," the father declared. "When did you send out the invitations?"

"The day before yesterday."

"The day before yesterday," he repeated mildly. "If it was the day before yesterday, then some people haven't even seen them yet." He spoke as though this was undoubtedly the most important reason.

Then, just as he was saying that it was late and we'd better start, Tsumura, the young owner of Tsunokuniya, walked in looking extremely serious and dressed in very proper formal robes. We exchanged glances in greeting. Tsumura was the only guest from my side, but I heaved a sigh of relief as I introduced him to Tomoko's father and that served as a signal for the ceremony to finally begin. Everyone took their places at the table—then, as per the usual form, congratulations were offered and the introductions of the bride and groom completed. The ceremony went off smoothly, but when I looked around for Tsumura I couldn't find him anywhere. "I'll just go with you to your house and see if everything's ready." The mother sounded very relieved as she rode with Tomoko and me in the car. We did not talk as we drove along the dark Keihin Highway. Each of us was well aware of how we'd become entangled in this peculiar state of affairs, but no one said a word.

At the top of the hill the house came into view and I could see lights shining like Christmas ornaments in every window. During our absence the maid, who worked for Tomoko and would be employed at our house, had come from their Senzoku home and set things in order.

"Have you finished?" the mother asked when the maid walked out to meet us.

After we took off our shoes and went in, I saw that the house had been thoroughly fixed up. In fact, I, who had left just half a day before, could not believe it was the same place. The furniture I'd scraped together from the used furniture shops just two or three days previously looked settled in, as if the pieces had been there for a long time. The drawing room was well heated by the gas stove and fresh flowers bloomed on the tables. The bath was ready. The house had an absolutely natural feeling to it, as if lived in for many months. When I looked around an unutterably strange feeling filled my soul, for in half a day the warm atmosphere of that house in Senzoku had come flowing into my own residence. This was what a home was supposed to be and in a home it made no difference what the husband thought or what was on the wife's mind, just as long as one lived peacefully, wrapped in a great warmth. My musings had gone this far when the maid served us hot tea.

"Well, I must be going. I don't want to be in your way," the mother said and soon departed.

When the two of us were finally alone, Tomoko seemed gloomy. "What's the matter?" I asked her gently.

She changed into a white nightgown and lay down on the bed, peering fixedly into the distance with a dark look in her eyes. I could imagine what she was thinking. She had worked herself up like any young woman, anticipating the ceremony in a way that bore no relation to what had actually transpired. In her ideal wedding, she would be marrying Yuasa Jōji, a contemporary artist returned from a stay abroad. She would be marrying Yuasa Jōji, whose character she had never bothered to investigate but who was, above all, the famous Yuasa Jōji. She had counted on the many celebrities who would attend and probably also dreamed of the next morning's newspaper where there would doubtless be a big picture of Tomoko smiling behind her bouquet. The troupe of her school friends had come to see just that Tomoko in all her glory. And after rehashing those scenes, Tomoko must have remembered the young student she had parted from at her house in Senzoku.

"What's the matter?" I asked again.

Tomoko looked at me with a dull expression in her eyes. "I'm very tired."

"Well, good night. You sleep late tomorrow morning." I spoke gently since I was already accustomed to my role as urbane husband. I stood up to pull the curtains shut and after after kissing Tomoko lightly on her feverish cheek, I turned off the lamp on the night table.

． ． ．

My life with Tomoko began the next day. It was a bright, clear day, as if the wedding ceremony and that young student had been completely forgotten. We went together to the house in Senzoku and once there were told that before leaving the father had asked us to go over to his office. Thus we had to set out again for Kyōbashi. When we reached his office the father was in high spirits and again introduced me to each of the important officials of the company who had come to the Josuikan the previous day.

"A modern and enlightened man like yourself will need these things to set up a new household," he proclaimed, opening the company's electric appliance and equipment catalogue on the table and placing a mark by each item. "I'll have them delivered to your house today." Then he called me to another room and told me he was worried about something he'd heard from Tomoko's mother concerning my former wife. "It may be rude of me to say this, but if the matter can be settled with a bit of money, I'm sure I can help you out. Also it might be good to clear things up in your family register and have your ex-wife's name removed. In any case, we have rowed our boat this far and so now we must maneuver our ship well."

"I don't think you need to worry," I answered evenly, suppressing a faint sense of uneasiness in my heart. "And even if there is some trouble, this really has nothing to do with you, Father. It's entirely my problem and I hope not to cause you any concern."

"Is that so? It makes me feel better to hear you say that." He still had a doubting look on his face, but perhaps because he didn't want Tomoko to know about that conversation, he quickly changed his mood and suggested that the three of us go to Mitsukoshi together. "Let's go shopping for your new home. It reminds me of the time twenty or thirty years ago when Yasuko and I used to go walking in America."

At Mitsukoshi he was the one who took charge of purchases, from cooking pots to the highest quality tempura equipment. Tomoko's father was evidently just delighted with his first experience of a daughter getting married and the two of us tried to match his gaiety. Our efforts were eventually rewarded for we did manage to feel the brightness of a newly married couple.

In the following days, our life together was more peaceful than I had expected. Tomoko was so cheerful that I thought I might have been mistaken about the young student. And I, as the urbane husband, did not forget to show my fondness for my young wife. This will do fine, I began thinking. If we can continue in this manner I'll become quite contented and perhaps gradually return to my work. For the first time in my life I had the kind of house where I could sit at peace by the stove and drink hot coffee. For a while I passed my time savoring that happiness, and my friends, who had at first kept their distance from my new life, saw that I was persisting in my contrary behavior. One by one they contacted us and our relations steadily returned to normal with frequent visits back and forth. Since we were often invited to go out dancing with Baba and his wife at the Imperial Hotel, we met there one night and as usual Baba danced with Tomoko and I danced with Baba's wife, Natsue. When I put my arm on Natsue's slender back, I could feel beneath the sheer fabric of her evening gown that she'd become so thin that her bones stuck out.

"You've really lost weight," I told her.

Natsue did not reply and then, sighing weakly, she said, "Tell me, Jōji, will you go with me? I haven't been feeling well lately."

"Where are you going?"

"Any place would be fine. Maybe to a hot springs or something like that. I'd like to go and relax for a while."

I could hear Natsue's quiet voice clearly, even against the loud jazz and the shuffling feet of the dancers. I had heard a rumor that Baba's household—because of the freedom which made it unlike a real household—would soon split up, since Baba had recently become preoccupied with a new young love. That night, too, the girlfriend had come along with the husband and wife, and so Natsue's low sigh was perhaps a lament for the atmosphere in her house. But by nature Natsue took pride in her free habits and I didn't think that she was about to go into mourning over her husband's new romance.

"A hot springs is a good idea," I answered noncommittally. "Tomoko has also been feeling out of sorts. Maybe we could all go together." I forgot to mention this, but since Tomoko had come to live with me she occasionally told me that she was feeling ill and visited the doctor. Her cousin worked at a research center for infectious diseases and every three days or so she went there. When she returned she looked very weak and threw herself on the bed, too tired to talk. Then the next day she would immediately be better and hurry me out for some amusement like dancing. But I thought it might do her health some good if we left Tokyo for a hot springs in the country.

Returning in the taxi, Tomoko started talking about Natsue. "You certainly danced as if you're very good friends."

I brought up the conversation about the trip to the hot springs. "She was wondering if we could all go together. Would you enjoy that? We could all have a good time together. It might perk up your spirits."

"You really don't catch on to things too well, do you?" she snapped, turning a glistening eye toward me. "When she says she wants to go together, she's trying to say that the two of you should go by yourselves." Then she fell into an extremely bad mood.

From that time on, the disgruntled look on Tomoko's face became even more noticeable. By nature she didn't talk much but within her quiet manner there had been a gentleness that won people over. After that discussion in the taxi, however, she was perpetually sullen and silent. We'd been together for less than two months but I thought I knew what had brought about this change in Tomoko. She had stuffed herself full of a young girl's gay illusions about her life with me and inevitably that daydreaming had to end in disillusionment.

One day, I was making a leisurely return home when I saw my ex-wife, Matsuyo, on the porch, arguing with Tomoko. Tomoko was saying that I wasn't home and that she should come back again some other day, but Matsuyo insisted that she didn't want to leave and would stand there until my return. In the time required for me to be taken aback by this, Matsuyo turned around and saw me. I paid no attention and continued walking.

"Well, anyway," I muttered, "why don't you come in?"

"I was just about to be turned out," Matsuyo retorted.

I looked with contempt at Matsuyo, who was wearing thick makeup. Her cheeks drew up into a twitch of a smile. Then I spoke to Tomoko, "We're going to talk. Go and wait in the sitting room."

"No." Tomoko looked pale and drawn. "No, I want to listen also."

Accepting the situation seemed wisest and soon we all faced each other in the drawing room. "What was it that you wanted to talk about?" I asked Matsuyo.

"Quite a nice house you have, isn't it?" Matsuyo observed, passing her eyes over the piano with its display of dolls, the burning gas stove, and the curtains. "Here you are living like some lord and I'm in a rat's nest."

"Is that so?" I scoffed. "Just because you live in a rat's nest, does it mean I have to also? You had something to talk to me about. What is it?"

"I'm here about that little item you were going to give me."

"Going to give you?" Without thinking, I began to shout. "Those matters are already settled. You've already agreed to them. Now what are you talking about?"

"What proof do you have?" Matsuyo spoke in a cold, hushed voice.

Proof? Only then did I understand what had brought Matsuyo there. She meant that she and I had only verbally agreed that I would give her fifty yen per month. We hadn't yet exchanged any legal documents.

"If you start talking nonsense, you'll get yourself into real trouble." I was determined to remain in control. "If you don't like the agreement we made, we'll just forget about it. That will be fine with me."

"I won't let you threaten me. The situation has completely changed since then. Yes, it certainly has changed. Before, you didn't even have enough money to take a train ride to Tokyo and now you've married this rich girl. It's like the difference between night and day. Did you think I was so deceived, that I was keeping quiet until now because I intended to follow meekly whatever you said? Did you think I had gone crying off to sleep after being deceived like that? I am not so good-natured."

"I am already aware of that. But just for your information, let me tell you something. I may have married a rich girl but that doesn't mean I've become rich. And tell me, how many thousands of yen do you want?"

I meant this sarcastically, but Matsuyo, who was surprisingly simpleminded, took me seriously. "Let me think," she pondered and the hardened expression on her face abruptly dissolved into a smile. "You know, I investigated. I found out what kind of family Tomoko comes from and the reason you married her. So I understand everything. I want ten thousand yen."

"You must be joking," I answered, disgusted. "I can't give you a thousand yen, much less ten thousand. You'd better resign yourself to that. When you come here and talk like this, you really are your mother's daughter." Matsuyo's mother, who loved lawsuits, had already died, but she had been so preoccupied with her legal affairs while alive that, according to the rumors, she had been in constant contact with her lawyers throughout her life. Matsuyo had also laughed about her mother's ways in the past. Only anger made me talk like this.

"That's fine. I'm happy to be my mother's daughter." Matsuyo turned pale, dragging her chair around to face Tomoko. "Since that's the way you feel, I'll just talk to Tomoko. Tomoko—I'm a brazen women who can calmly say these things, but I think you can sympathize with me. You didn't think this man was just a bachelor, did you? You knew all about me and the child and still you got married, didn't you?"

"You idiot!" I yelled at her before I really knew what I was doing. "What's the point of bringing that up? If you want the money that badly then file a lawsuit! A lawsuit or whatever you want! You know, listening to this shameless woman has made me tired. Get out! And don't come back here again!"

As if by reflex, Matsuyo picked up her shawl and stood up. While backing out, she sneered, "I suppose something that hurts really does hurt, doesn't it? And don't give me that threatening look. You can leer as long as you like, but it won't help." She poured all her hate into this parting shot and then, having finished her speech, she left.

Once Matsuyo had gone, Tomoko went into the sitting room, threw herself down on the bed and cried her eyes out.

"You should realize," I pleaded with her, "that she may talk like that, but there's nothing she can really do. She only likes to hear herself talk. Why, I thought you'd laugh at such foolishness . . ."

"But . . ." Tomoko didn't lift her head and just continued to sob. "The legality of it, that's the most important thing."

"What do you mean, 'legality'?" I was nonplused and spoke to her as if I were humoring a child. "Is that what you're worried about? If that's what's troubling you, I'll settle all that for you right now. I was just confused and surprised to see you become so obstinate all of a sudden . . ."

"No, that's not . . . No, I . . ." Tomoko became even more morose and continued to cry, her shoulders shaking.

As I looked at her loose, wavy hair and slender shoulders, I realized that Tomoko was not crying because Matsuyo had come and delivered that lecture. She was complaining about her entire life with me. The discontent had not taken on any clear form until Matsuyo appeared to give it a shape. I told myself that I had nothing to worry about, and in fact Tomoko's sadness frightened me less than any analysis I might have made of the reasons behind it. Thus I hastily put the whole matter out of my mind. Had I broken down over such a small matter, I would never have crossed over that dangerous bridge. A dangerous bridge—but what was the purpose of that bridge? Couldn't one say that once the bridge was crossed, there would be a safety zone on the other side? But whatever I've done in my life, I've always stopped short of crossing that dangerous bridge. Once these grim ruminations surfaced, the disgust and anger I felt toward Matsuyo shot through me again. What did I care about my so-called unjust behavior toward Matsuyo? I didn't even want to pay the monthly alimony, not to mention the thousands of yen for consolation money. What reason did I have to pay money to a woman I had grown to hate? Those elemental questions raged through me.

The next day I went to a pet shop on a Ginza back street to look at a dog that Tomoko had admired, and upon my return I glanced over at the dining room terrace, which stood behind a low hedge and was visible from the street. There, with his back to me, was a tall young student in uniform, standing and talking to Tomoko. I saw right away that he was the Keiō student whom I had forgotten about for a while. I started whistling and went around from the the side door to the garden.

Somewhat flustered, Tomoko introduced me to the boy. "He's a friend of Kuni's," she explained, meaning her brother Kunio. She spoke for the boy, saying that he'd been passing by and so had dropped in for a brief visit. I gathered that he'd come before when I wasn't around.

"Well, why don't you come in?" I assumed a genial manner and went in first, leading the boy into the parlor. There we made friendly conversation about nothing very important until he remembered that he had to meet a friend and left in haste. "He's an interesting boy, isn't he?" I spoke rather straightforwardly, but Tomoko only looked up at me without replying.

I know anyone would find this strange, but I honestly had come to value my life with Tomoko, whom I did not think I really loved at all. I certainly wasn't going to allow any problems regarding Matsuyo to get in my way, and even if Tomoko had some feelings inappropriate to a wife, I didn't want to disrupt our lives over them. I insist upon the seriousness of my position here, which was completely different from the attitude of that urbane and know-it-all husband I once thought myself to be. I liked the house. No, let me put it another way—I, who had long lived an insecure life buffeted by waves, loved the house with its warm stoves like a sailor who had finally reached a harbor. Afterwards I understood that this stance, when all was said and done, only expressed my own selfishness.

It happened on an unusually warm, clear winter day that Tomoko and I were drinking our usual coffee after a late breakfast. We had opened the sunroom curtains to look out onto the terrace, and beyond the hedge a pretty young woman slowly passed by. At first I could only vaguely make out her bright violet kimono and crimson obi, but when she turned to face me quietly, coming to a place where I could see her from my seat, I let out a low cry of surprise and put down my cup. It was Tsuyuko. Without a doubt Tsuyuko's eyes with their long eyelashes were looking at me. The kimono and obi were certainly the same ones I had seen her wear before. Startled, I left my seat. Tomoko, who had her back to the street, gave me a questioning look but I had already run out the front door to chase after Tsuyuko. Once outside, I stopped. Where had she gone? She must have walked from the hilltop to this street, so she couldn't have gone more than half a block. I ran up to the wooden wall at the corner several houses ahead, but didn't see her. I hesitated and stood there for a moment—then, since the road divided in two, I took one fork down as far as the railway crossing and again retraced my steps, going along a narrow street that led out onto another part of town. I hadn't found Tsuyuko anywhere. Perhaps I'd lost her on one of the side streets.

But what was Tsuyuko doing there anyway? I stood in the road in my slippers and tried to quiet my heaving breath. Tsuyuko had been there! Tsuyuko—who was supposed to have taken the boat on November 4th from Kobe to America—was still in Japan. Was it possible? Gradually I started to doubt my own eyes. Four months had passed since that time and I had reestablished myself in a completely different world, had indeed vowed that I would not recall Tsuyuko even in my dreams. It was only my stupidity that made me believe I had seen her so clearly, I told myself, laughing and finally returning to my usual state. But the next afternoon when I returned home, Tomoko was out and on the desk in the sitting room was a telegram, unmistakably from Tsuyuko.

TOMORROW MORNING AT TEN. WAITING AT SHIBUYA STATION.
TSUYUKO

I held that telegram for a long time, my hand shaking. Tsuyuko was in Japan after all. She was in Japan and had passed by the house the previous day in order to see me.

"Tsune." I called the maid. "Has Tomoko seen this telegram?"

"No, sir," she answered clearly. "The young lady only put it on the desk. She seemed in a hurry and went out."

This maid who had come with Tomoko from the house in Senzoku always referred to Tomoko as "the young lady."

"Is that so?" I spoke without a trace of alarm, but the fold in the telegram was different from what it had been when first sent out and therefore I knew that Tomoko had read the message. But what did that mean? Completely off balance, I had only inquired about Tomoko in order to be convinced that I still had my wits about me. By then I could not think of the house or Tomoko. Ah, Tsuyuko is in Japan! I wanted to raise my voice and shout, but under that cry of jubilation I could also hear the sounds of the collapse of this peaceful household I had finally created for myself. In any case, what were my choices? Even if the warm fires from the stoves could have held me back, I don't know how much I would have wanted to stay on in that house. For I no longer knew what I thought—the only thing I did know was that the next morning at ten, I'd go to meet Tsuyuko and that meeting would probably mark the end of Tomoko and our house.

· · ·

The next day I met Tsuyuko after half a year. Perhaps it was her blue coat, but she looked ill—not only was she thinner than before, there was also a blue, almost transparent shadow on her slender neck and the sides of her cheeks. Only her eyes were surprisingly large. Her unfortunate appearance, so like a doll that had been crushed, awakened my sleeping passion once more. The love I had felt for Tsuyuko six months before returned with the same frenzy and intensity, and I saw that I would do anything not to lose her again. My life with Tomoko, by comparison, had lost whatever value it once possessed. Despite my desire for Tsuyuko, she looked at me with eyes indescribably hollow and empty of any interest in life. Like a person half dead, she murmured over and over, "I want to die." She had faith in my love, she said, but couldn't believe it had any chance of surviving in the real world. Nor did I have the strength to return her to the realm of the living.

She told me that she had in fact gone to America from Kobe as planned, but even during the two months that she lived abroad she had incessantly pursued the thought of death until at last she returned to Japan. I told her to give me three days. After that brief meeting, which hadn't even lasted two hours, I had no desire to return home and so I went out by myself to walk in a daze until nightfall. I too had been drawn into that world-weary mood of Tsuyuko's and, while I had specifically told her to wait for three days, my mind wasn't yet able to think about how I would free myself from my immediate situation in that time. As I walked, my only companion was the headlong, shuddering sound of my present life being destroyed. The form that destruction would take, however, did not come to me. If I'm not careful, I thought, I too will be possessed by the gods of misfortune—I forced myself to consider Tsuyuko's state of mind in that ironic manner to regain my composure. When I reached home, Tomoko as usual wasn't in, probably because she had gone to the hospital that day. I ate dinner by myself.

"What time did she go out?" I asked the maid.

"Just after you," Tsune answered, rather abashed.

Tsune had come to the house with Tomoko on the day of the wedding. To be sure, the table where I ate my dinner, the napkin, the chest of drawers, the bed, the piano—every single one of those things Tomoko had brought with her. The only objects that could be called mine were the old chair and table I'd purchased from the neighborhood second-hand furniture store the day before my wedding, a few books, and the materials in my studio. It was odd to recognize that I'd lived among those things until that very morning without the slightest qualm. The interior of the house felt uncomfortable, unfamiliar, and I kept wondering what had driven me to live there convinced that it was my own home. Perhaps my life had reached such an extremity that until the previous day I'd forced myself to believe that I'd do anything to continue my existence there. I secluded myself in the sitting room to mull over the mystery of how Tomoko and I had each chosen an utterly unsuitable partner. We had walked into an outrageous mistake but were too afraid to bring our life together to a quick end. Soon after, the clock struck eight and then nine but Tomoko didn't return. Although she had been going out every day, saying that she was headed to the hospital, she'd never returned so late.

As I walked into the bedroom, I was thinking that perhaps she'd gone to the house in Senzoku when I noticed Tomoko's old handbag lying slightly open on top of the mirror stand. Two letters were sticking out and I idly picked them up—one, from her old classmate Maeda Tomie, who had married a naval officer in Kure, and the other, a discarded version of Tomoko's reply. Before I even realized what I was doing, I read the letters. Tomie had written in detail about how boring her married life was and how her young dreams had completely vanished. She wrote that her husband was nothing but a fat Don Quixote who only liked to eat good food. Tomoko's reply, however, spoke from the other side of the fence. She wrote about the pleasures of her marriage—how in the morning her gentle husband always brought her a cup of chocolate with warm milk when she was still lying in bed, and at night many young guests came to the house. Her husband would sit on the sofa, put her on his knees, and sing her songs. At that time, some of the young women who had taken to American ways liked using the English word *me* to describe themselves. She had filled up a whole page writing about her husband as "the person who belongs to *me*."

I actually thought I'd burst out laughing, for none of those scenes had occurred in our life together. Most likely, Tomoko had only tried to write about images from a movie she'd seen somewhere, and since this was probably her vision of a perfect married life I couldn't help but see an almost comic pathos in the whole situation. During the months that we'd lived together, we'd smiled at each other but when alone our eyes looked off into different worlds. "She's just a child, you know," her father had recently said of Tomoko—"I know it's troublesome for you, but do me a favor and treat her very fondly, humor her as if she were a kitten just weaned from her mother." This was exactly the sort of letter that a kitten would write, but I myself had seen no signs of Tomoko acting like a pampered kitten. If indeed she had such feelings, Tomoko had hidden them all deep within her heart.

—But come to think of it, where had she gone wandering off to, this late at night? I looked at the clock near my pillow once more and saw that it was past ten. If she'd stopped at the house in Senzoku, they should already have sent her home. Then I understood—since Tomoko had definitely read the telegram from Tsuyuko the previous morning, hadn't she anticipated what was going to happen next and left the house? No doubt I had analyzed the situation correctly. As I considered this turn of events, my mind went numb. Yes, Tomoko had run away. If that's what has happened, well, is there any reason to complain, I wondered. Hadn't matters turned out just as I wished, I told myself. I had told Tsuyuko to give me three days, but in less than that time, within the very same day, Tomoko had destroyed our life together without requiring me to lift a finger. Wasn't that what I had wanted? I listened to the sound of the wind blowing outside and my soul stirred, imagining what had happened to Tsuyuko. I tried to recall Tsuyuko's appearance when we parted, but my worry about Tomoko kept coming back, brushing aside such visions. Irritation took hold of me and when the clock struck twelve I got up, still in my pajamas, and went out the back way to the public phone to call the Senzoku house.

"What did you say? She hasn't come home yet?" Tomoko's mother, who had been sleeping when I called, was extremely distressed. "What should we do? Where could she have gone? When she left here this evening, she was jubilant, very happy."

She became greatly flustered in her alarm and I could vividly picture the scene as she called out to wake up her husband while the maids added to the confusion. The mother returned to the phone to ask me to come over there right away. I immediately caught a passing taxi and raced over to Senzoku. Everyone was asleep in the other houses, but within that deep stillness I could see a distant light from Tomoko's father's study where they waited.

"This is just terrible." The father started to speak in a voice heavy with worry as soon as I arrived. "We thought you and she had gone to Atami again."

"On her way back she was going to stop at Matsuyo's place," the mother added.

"At Matsuyo's?" I was stunned as I repeated what she had said, for I never expected to hear those words from the mother's lips.

It seemed that after Matsuyo had paid her unexpected visit to our house, Tomoko had, at times unknown to me, met her on two or three occasions. And that very day, Tomoko had spoken to her parents about how if Matsuyo received five hundred yen, the matter would be settled without further trouble. Tomoko had therefore asked her parents to lend her that sum of money. When Matsuyo had come to our house, her parting remarks had been threatening— she wouldn't remove her name from my family register unless she received ten thousand yen. What could have induced Matsuyo to agree to settle everything for only five hundred yen? Although on second thought I realized that Matsuyo was capable of such behavior, I still couldn't stand the thought of Tomoko going to Senzoku to borrow the money.

"And you gave her the money?"

"I have some stock certificates that I put aside for her when she was a child. She said she was going to go with you to live in a warm place for a while and so she went home with about one thousand yen, to cover the expenses for both."

Since Tomoko and I had not discussed any plans for a trip recently, she had doubtless taken the money and fled. Or perhaps she had acted on her words and gone to Matsuyo's house. Without even bothering to sit down I had them call me a taxi.

"As soon as you find out something, you'll call, won't you?" the mother pleaded, coming out to the car. "You will come back here again, won't you?"

In fact, the more it dawned on me that Tomoko had run off somewhere, the more I longed for blood. Matsuyo lived in the same house she had moved to with the child when she had separated from me, before I left Kamata. Since I had gone there to help transport her things, finding my way in the daylight would have presented no difficulty, but the house was located on a crowded, reclaimed marshland and in the darkness I had no idea where it was. After the taxi went around in circles several times, I became so irritated that I finally got out of the car at a narrow street. There was still a light on in a house beside a vacant lot further back and I called through the window.

"Does Takahashi Matsuyo live around here?"

"Her place is behind this one."

I could see a veranda directly opposite, still brightly lit so late at night. I tiptoed forward and approached the veranda, staying in its dark shadow and making my way past several long, scraggly cypresses in the garden. I looked to see if Tomoko's shoes were there before going into the house, but I couldn't find them. I was sure that Tomoko would hide if she knew I had come and so I approached quietly, drawing my body up against the wall. The sliding door was illuminated by the lights within—I quickly reached out and hurled it open.

"You really are so rude!" Matsuyo spoke shrilly, her face in white makeup ready to confront me.

Behind her a man wearing a quilted robe sat by the brazier drinking. I recognized Okano, whom I'd met several times before on his frequent visits to the house in Kamata. He was a reporter for the local news section of the *Tokyo Evening Newspaper* and was supposed to be some distant relative of Matsuyo's. Since I hadn't expected to find him there so late at night, drinking at the home of a woman who lived by herself, my displeasure was apparent.

"What's rude about it?"

"Don't you think you're rude, opening the door like that without even knocking?"

"Tomoko's here, isn't she?"

"You're asking me about Tomoko? It's hardly likely that she would come here." A faint mocking smile rose to her lips, thick with lipstick. "This must really be a lot of trouble for you, coming out in the middle of the night to look for your wife."

"Yuasa-san, don't just stand there like that. Come on in." Even Okano spoke with familiarity while settling a big grin on his greasy face. Matsuyo snickered as she glanced at Okano.

"Shall we tell him?"

"There's nothing to hide, is there?"

"Well," Matsuyo laughed again, obviously enjoying herself, "to tell you the truth, Tomoko was here until just a little while ago. She says that she's sick and tired of living with you."

"She came here? Then where did she go?"

"Why ask me where she went? Isn't she fast asleep in your house right now?"

Barely able to suppress a sudden wildness boiling up in my throat, I tried to remain as calm as possible. "I think I can do without your sarcasm right now. Do you have any idea where she was planning to go? If she kills herself, I don't know what I'll do."

"Now that would be a real scoop for the evening newspaper!" Okano proclaimed.

No sooner had Okano spoken than Matsuyo said, "Did you say that she was going to commit suicide?" And into her narrow eyes there rose a look of utter disdain. "You really are conceited, aren't you? Even now, with the rope practically around your neck, you can't get rid of your vanity, can you? You must be joking, thinking that Tomoko is going to kill herself because of you. She's in love with somebody else, you know."

Her words pierced my very core and I felt myself reeling from the shock. But, I told myself, perhaps Matsuyo had just made up this fanciful tale to exact her revenge, to provoke me. Death at that moment would have been more acceptable to me than revealing any sign of distress. Nevertheless, Matsuyo's scornful smile had sapped me of any nerve to retaliate. The image before me wasn't Matsuyo's sneer, or Okano's grin. What I saw, like a figure gradually emerging from a drawing done with invisible ink, was that tall student in the Keiō uniform. Had she fled with that boy? There could no longer be the slightest doubt about it. I had a clear vision of him leaning up against our dining room terrace as he talked with Tomoko. Come to

107

think of it, since the time just after I first met Tomoko, I'd seen him on enough occasions to wonder what was going on, and once my suspicions were aroused it didn't take much effort to figure out the kind of relationship they had. But even so, I had half-pretended not to see anything, as if by design. If, in the worst possible case, Tomoko was indeed that boy's lover, I would calmly go about my business, pretending not to notice, because I was certain my love for Tomoko did not extend beyond a very cool, calculated feeling. Yet if I had such control over myself, why was I getting so excited? I tried to regain my composure as these thoughts assailed me, but I realized my very efforts would only send Matsuyo and her companion into more of their derisive laughter and would serve no purpose. So I retreated to where I had asked the taxi to wait, leaving their jeering behind. Afterwards I learned that Tomoko had still been at Matsuyo's that night, had heard me ask for directions at the house in back, and upon recognizing my voice, had turned pale, crying, "Yuasa is here." They had then urged her to hide in the closet.

When I returned home I called Tsune into the sitting room to ask her about Tomoko. "She has disappeared. I'd like you to tell me everything you know about this."

Tsune looked down without speaking.

"If you don't tell me right away," I continued, "there will be some very foolish mistakes made. If you leave out even one small thing, you won't be doing her a favor."

"I should . . ." Tsune tried to speak but instead burst into sobs. Her honest nature set her to weeping for some time since she apparently feared that she had been the cause of the uproar. "You must excuse me, but actually four or five days ago I mailed a postcard."

"What postcard?"

"I wasn't sure what it meant but it said something like, 'I have decided to go with you. Please wait at Tokyo Station.' "

"That was all? You mailed that postcard?"

"No. After that, the night before last, I sent a telegram."

"What telegram?"

"It said, 'I can't go tomorrow morning. Please forgive me. Letter follows.' "

"You sent that telegram the night before last?"

It then came back to me that on the particular night she described Tomoko had announced after dinner that she had to get up very early the next morning. A music teacher from her school days, whom she admired, was going back to the country and she wanted to see him off. When I asked her what time the train left, she said it was the 7:40 express. I told her that if she was going to see him off on such an early train she would have to wake up at five in the morning and would still have to rush. I suggested that she was not strong enough to get up so early, offhandedly making her see the foolishness of the whole idea and putting an end to her plans. Her scheme squelched, Tomoko had gone off grumbling. Even then, she had already planned to leave the next morning. It wasn't that she had seen Tsuyuko's telegram and in a tempestuous mood had decided to leave the house. She had methodically made her plans before that.

"Do you know where Kurota's house in Nishikoyama is?" For the first time I uttered that boy's name.

"Yes. I went with the young lady once when she was living in the other house."

"Then you'll know approximately where it is, won't you? Get ready. We'll go together right away."

Although it was past two in the morning, I went with Tsune by taxi to Nishikoyama and together we searched out Kurota's older sister's house, where he was living. The house, with a crude Western-style drawing room stuck on, looked like the kind of rented dwelling that could be found in any suburb. Built compactly behind a small hill on the outskirts of town, it had a garden with a lawn. When I rang the doorbell several times, the sound echoed through the house and even outside. In a moment a female voice asked for our names and then a tall, thin woman, who must have been the older sister, came out.

"Is Kurota-kun here?" I inquired.

The sister raised a surprised, suspicious face to my question as her worry instantly surfaced. "Gorō went back to our home in the country two mornings ago. But please, do come in."

I didn't budge as I told her about Tomoko's disappearance. The sister was much surprised and unable to speak for some time. "I am pretty sure he went back home to the country two mornings ago," she stated succinctly. "I can't believe that my timid brother would do such a thing."

In the morning she'd make inquiries at their home in Hiroshima and would inform us by noon, she hoped, about the reply. After that I went straight to the house in Senzoku. When I reported what had happened, without concealing any details, the mother of course turned pale. She probably knew more about the Kurota affair than I did.

"You must forgive us." The father looked very contrite. "I don't know what she is intending to do."

"And you were so good," the mother said, "to marry her after we had insisted so . . ."

This good-hearted couple, their sorrow genuine, thus ascribed everything, from first to last, to their daughter's selfishness. By then I had a vague inkling of Tomoko's state of mind. She had been seeing Kurota since before she knew me, but when I appeared I entertained her with my clever talk. She loved Kurota but her curiosity about me got the better of her. My photograph sometimes appeared in the newspapers and she started imagining that I led a very exciting life. Just like the young girls who wear themselves out trying to get the Malay baseball players' signatures, she longed to marry me, no matter what the difficulties were. Foremost among those difficulties was what happened on the wedding day, when she met Kurota just as she was about to go to the hall. This is only what I imagined, but Tomoko must have told Kurota then that she was about to marry someone she didn't care for, simply to please her parents. Of course, she would not have failed to assure him that this had nothing to do with her true feelings. And in fact, didn't I see her relating this sad tale while weeping and lamenting about how they must part? For Tomoko, marriage was like a label stuck on the outside of a tin can—it didn't matter what was inside, but the outside definitely had to be bright, cheerful, pleasant. Yet our wedding ceremony itself had been wrapped in ambiguities she could not begin to comprehend, and our married life, which was supposed to have been so gay—well, it goes without saying that no one from the ladies' magazines came to interview her for her thoughts on marital bliss. Instead, my ex-wife came for money and our days were filled with gloom. It was ironic that Tomoko had tried to write a letter to her friend singing about her happy life.

Then Tomoko's restlessness intensified and she considered ways to rebuild her life. She had even gone to see Matsuyo. But when she met disappointment at every turn, she thought she might as well flee with Kurota. She thought she could at least catch me off my guard in that way. That's as far as she had gone in her thinking when the telegram from Tsuyuko arrived. Seeing the telegram, Tomoko was clever enough to realize that if she did not leave, probably I would. She determined to get away first. I felt that my analysis of her state of mind was at least seventy percent correct.

By the time I left Tomoko's parents and reached home, it was close to daybreak. I went into the bedroom and sat on the bed for a long time, stunned. Tomoko's red slippers were aligned at my feet and on the mirror stand were the letters I had read, left just as they had been the day before. By then those sheets of paper had taken Tomoko's place and seemed to pity me. I remembered the look on Matsuyo's face when she had said, *Even now, with the rope practically around your neck, you can't get rid of your vanity, can you?* It was clear that my fortunes had suffered a complete reversal in a few short hours and I had become a laughingstock. Was I going to let that happen? Never! But brooding had set my nerves on edge and I returned to the crux of the matter—I'd been duped by a mere girl. The more I tried to rid my mind of that conclusion, the more irritatingly it stuck there. To be perfectly objective about it, I had not been an honest and sincere husband to Tomoko and my feelings for her had never developed into a real love, but that had nothing to do with the fury that gripped me when I realized that Tomoko had moved out first. Even if I had to search heaven and earth, I'd find her. A great turbulence welled up within me, emotions equal to what I wished to express with that exaggerated vow. Yes, no matter how far away she had run, I would search for her. And when I found her, I would bring her back to the house and make her feel what I was feeling now . . . By then my anger had carried me past the bounds of reason, seizing my entire being with a palpable weight and force. The previous noon at the Kōbaiken I had decided that no matter what I had to sacrifice, I wouldn't be separated from Tsuyuko again, but I couldn't compare the intensity of that moment to what I experienced there at home. The strength of my emotions as I sat in our bedroom was beyond compare, enough to unsettle my whole existence.

In the morning, feeling somewhat drowsy, I waited for news about the reply to the telegram sent from Nishikoyama. Soon a messenger came to say that Kurota had not yet returned to his home in Hiroshima after all and that the Nishikoyama house would, just in case, investigate where he had gone and inform me right away. From this reply I saw that my speculations had turned out to be ninety percent correct. I immediately left the house and went to inquire at the homes of each of the friends Tomoko usually visited. It was already late at night when I finally went to the Akasaka apartment of Momoko, the girl with the bobbed hair who had come with Tomoko to Baba's studio the first time we had met. Momoko was still up, her room strewn with clothes, and she was standing in front of the mirror trying on a new hat she'd just bought that day.

"Ah, how awful. Is that what happened?" Momoko nodded her head in an exaggerated manner, revealing her instinctive delight in gossip. "Why don't you go and look at the Hibiya Hotel where Tatsuko was staying just the other day? I imagine that Tomoko's first stop would be at Tatsuko's. Tomoko has been visiting her practically every day." Tomoko's friend Tatsuko had gone back home to Shinshū to live but had recently visited Tokyo.

"She must have stopped there on her way home from the hospital every day," I surmised.

"The hospital?" Momoko started to laugh. "Really, Yuasa-san, did you honestly think she was going to a hospital? Don't you see that the hospital she was going to was Kurota?"

I smiled bitterly when I grasped the truth of this disclosure and how foolish my own naivete about the matter had been, for I'd seen Tomoko's condition when she came home from the hospital, always complaining that she was tired and taking a long nap on the sofa. The idea that she had gone to a rendezvous with Kurota each time produced a turmoil in my heart that I needn't try to describe. Even though our original motives hadn't been particularly bad, our whole marriage had turned into a mutual deception. So were we both to blame? It really had been both of us, I realized, as a wave of self-contempt rose up from within me. In any case, I decided to go to the Hibiya Hotel to see Tatsuko. Since it was too late in the evening to meet a young woman for the first time, I went home to wait until morning. When I did visit the hotel, I was told that Tatsuko had checked out four or five days ago.

"Could you show me the register?" I asked, keeping my tone casual. I passed a fifty-sen coin into the hand of the bellboy, who had appeared reluctant to show it to me. Once I got hold of the register I quickly flipped through the pages and found, in an entry two nights before, the name Ihara Toshiko written in a feminine hand that was clearly Tomoko's, alongside another woman's name. Tomoko had concealed her real name, Inoue Tomoko, but even in an emergency she hadn't been able to write a completely false name. The new name retained some of the old name's characters.

"Is this Ihara Toshiko still staying here?"

"Ihara-san left yesterday."

"Yesterday? Did she send any telegrams?"

"Yes, she did. I sent one."

"You? Do you remember what it said?"

The bellboy became suspicious and claimed that he didn't remember the message or the address. He eyed me with a sudden caution and so I stopped my investigation. I then went to the telegram section of the Kyōbashi Post Office, but when they also stubbornly refused my request I showed my card at the window. "My sister ran away from home two nights ago," I announced, formulating a plausible story about how I had asked the police to look for her, but since I was afraid of a suicide attempt I wanted to make the necessary arrangements for the search as quickly as possible. There apparently was a rule that they couldn't show their telegram file to anyone without a policeman present and for this reason would not do as I asked. Then a senior official who had heard this noisy exchange came out. After listening to me recite the facts once again, he became sympathetic enough to show me a pile of telegrams that had been clipped together. One was addressed to Kurota in what was unmistakably Tomoko's handwriting. He had apparently gone to some inn or rental cottage in Zushi.

LEAVING TONIGHT. TOMORROW MORNING TEN THIRTY-FOUR. PLEASE MEET ME AT KOBE STATION.

I looked at my wristwatch and saw that it was past eleven twenty-five. At about that time, if all had gone according to plan, Tomoko had already arrived at Kobe, met Kurota, who'd left from Zushi first, and together they were settling down in some hotel.

I offered my thanks and once out of the post office, I stopped at a pay phone to call the house in Senzoku. I asked for the mother. "I've discovered that she's in Kobe."

"Oh, that's good." She heaved a sigh.

"I'm going to Kobe. I have to pick up some things at home first, but if I can pack quickly I'll be able to make the two o'clock Fuji Express.

"Yes, by all means, please do that. But before you go, could you come here? There's something I must talk to you about."

If I didn't make the Fuji Express, there would be no more trains going west until the evening. I rushed back to Ōmori, stuffed some things into my bag, and was about to get into the taxi I had waiting outside when I remembered to ask Tsune if there had been any telegram from Tsuyuko. Tsuyuko—I hadn't had time to think about her for the past two days! No telegram had come. I told Tsune that if she received anything, she should have it forwarded to me at a private box at the Kobe Central Post Office. Then I hurried off to Senzoku.

. . .

Because of my phone call Tomoko's father had left his office and returned home.

"What should we do?" He was completely at a loss. "Do you think you should go by yourself or should her mother go along with you?"

They worried about their daughter, of course, but apparently were more afraid of the row that would result if I confronted Kurota and Tomoko on my own—just imagining the inevitable commotion seemed to fill them with dread.

"It's a terrible imposition on you, but once you bring Tomoko back I plan to do whatever is necessary to make this all up to you," the father told me. "All you have to do is bring her back—I want you to calm Tomoko down and get her to come home. If you meet and start shouting at each other, she'll feel as if she's been driven into a corner and then I don't know what foolish mistake she'll make next."

I too believed that it would be better to have the mother go along and once we agreed to that, the mother and I went to Tokyo Station. But just as I had feared, we could only get the night train.

"We'll be a full day late," the mother exclaimed, taking out her handkerchief and dabbing her eyes incessantly. "After we leave the station, where will we go? We're not going to ask the police for help, are we?"

"Family members are more useful than the police, I think. We'll still have to check at all the hotels, but there are only three or four that Tomoko would stay at in Kobe."

Her shoulders heaved as she drew a long breath. There weren't many passengers on that cold train and as the mother and I sat facing each other, our thoughts about Tomoko definitely ran in opposite directions. The mother only prayed that her daughter would be alive, but in my heart other emotions were gathering like storm-clouds.

We arrived in Kobe a few minutes after nine the next morning, took a taxi into town, then went to inquire at the Oriental Hotel and the Toa Hotel. Finally we went to the Suwayama Hotel and on the guest register discovered the same alias, Ihara Toshiko, next to a man's name, which seemed to be Kurota's.

"Here they are. Are these people still staying here?"

"No. They left this morning."

"What time this morning?"

"Just a little while ago. I think their car must have returned by now. Hey, has number six come back?"

The desk clerk called to a bellboy and had him search for the driver, who turned out to be at the taxi stand outside the front door. The driver recalled that he had taken them from the hotel to the foreign settlement area, eventually dropping them off at the foreigner's cemetery. No one had any idea where they had gone after that.

"What should we do now?" I muttered to myself. I cursed my luck, for if I'd taken that Fuji train the previous day at noon I would have been able to find Tomoko that night. Or, if we hadn't gone to the other hotels first, they would still have been here. I knew they were in Kobe but hadn't any idea where they were likely to go. Completely confused, we stood in the hotel entranceway.

"I think that sooner or later they plan to take a train for Shimonoseki," Tomoko's mother suggested.

"I don't know." I was still unable to judge.

Since they didn't take the taxi directly to the train station but got out in the foreign settlement area, perhaps they decided to take a boat somewhere and went to the wharf. Would they have gone go to Korea or to Shanghai? Or if not, did they intend to go to Beppu? They had about one thousand yen on them, and if they intended to wander about until that money ran out, we'd never be able to find them. We rehashed every single detail, deciding to go to the station after all and see if they had boarded one of the trains. But which train station—Kobe or Sannomiya? Wouldn't Tomoko instinctively leave from Kobe Station since she had met Kurota there in the first place? Without any logical way to come to a decision, I resorted to the old trick that seems made for such occasions—I took out a silver coin from my pocket and threw it on the floor. The coin came up Sannomiya and so off we went to Sannomiya Station. There were still several trains going west and we sat in the corner of the waiting room, trying not to attract attention, since any minute a taxi carrying the two of them might drive up. This possibility possessed me as I stared out at a corner of the plaza in front of the station, but no one resembling them appeared. Eventually the street lights came on and the roads grew dark. We had probably waited at the wrong spot. But my fatigue made me reluctant to think about these problems any more. After going through the strain of the past two days without any sleep, my body felt as flaccid as a wad of cotton, and with my mind muddled I turned to completely different matters, even considered going back to Tokyo without wasting any more time. The flickering red flames in the waiting room stove stung my tired eyes as I wondered what purpose had been served by coming all that distance to chase after some woman who had gone off with another man.

"I have to go to the post office for a moment," I informed the mother just after we had taken turns having dinner at the restaurant in front of the station.

"The post office?" The mother raised her swollen eyes.

I told her that there might be a message from Tokyo and she naturally assumed it was in regard to Tomoko. Actually, at that point it was less my concern about Tsuyuko than that I had sat opposite the mother for the whole day and needed a brief respite.

At the post office I did find a telegram from Tsuyuko, which said that she would be waiting at Shimbashi Station the next morning at eleven. If I went back on the last train that night I'd be there in time, I thought, a sudden desire to see Tsuyuko sailing through my heart like a cloud in the heavens. Then an unbearable, feverish need to see her gripped my whole being—the longing came upon me utterly without warning and was much the same as the pent-up feeling of a child away from home who longs for his mother. On my way back to the station, I thought that if we found Tomoko that night I could go back to Tokyo right away, and for that reason above all I prayed that Tomoko and her boyfriend would appear.

When I came back, the mother got up from where she had been anxiously sitting. "Did something come?"

I told her that there had been no news.

The mother walked quickly toward the ticket window. "Let's go to Hiroshima after all. I think if we go there, we'll discover something. I can't stand waiting here any longer."

While I was still trying to make up my mind, Tomoko's mother went ahead and bought two tickets. I stood there in a state of total indecision.

"That's the last train." The mother urged me forward.

We could hear the loudspeaker announcing the opening of the ticket gate for the train to Shimonoseki and I followed behind her as if by reflex, still of half a mind to leave her and catch the train in the opposite direction to Tokyo. Yet at last I found myself being dragged aboard the last train going west. As the train lurched forward, I told myself that I really had no other choice and became resigned to the inevitability of a trip to Hiroshima. Then a conductor came through and I called him over to ask for a blank telegram—I had to inform Tsuyuko that I wouldn't be able to return on time. I hurried off to the coffee shop in the next car to find a place to write where the mother wouldn't see me, but once there confusion reigned again.

I'VE COME TO KOBE ON EMERGENCY BUSINESS AND WILL BE
UNABLE TO RETURN BY TOMORROW. LET'S MEET THE DAY AFTER
TOMORROW AT SHIMBASHI STATION AT ELEVEN O'CLOCK.

I considered this message, but could I safely send such a telegram to Tsuyuko's house? If I sent it and the telegram got into the hands of some other member of the household, another disaster like the last time might ensue. Wasn't it wiser not to send the telegram and just see what happened in the morning?

I still had not made up my mind when I happened to look up and saw the backs of a young couple in Western clothes who had left their seats on the other side of the door just next to me to walk toward the dining car. They were the very image of Tomoko and Kurota. I automatically stood up and went after them. No question, it was Tomoko all right. I remembered that black astrakhan coat with the thick fur collar and her well-shaped legs and the way she walked, kicking up her toes as she went along. The two of them took seats in the middle of the dining car and sat down facing each other. The boy took a cigarette out of his pocket and lit it. Kurota, I remembered, had used just that gesture when we had talked for a few minutes in our parlor at home. I hesitated, unable to move, while I considered my alternatives. The restaurant's galley was within the partitioned section just beside me and the cook in his white uniform was silently peeling a fruit while he stared at me. Obviously it would not have been sensible to start shouting right then and there. Tomoko and Kurota had only to realize that I was riding in the same car before we'd find ourselves in the middle of a huge uproar. So instead of rushing over and abusing them with a few foul phrases I happened to have at hand, I hid myself behind the galley and tried to avoid Kurota's eye as he puffed on his cigarette. Peculiarly enough, I felt no trace of the violent fury I had been harboring for the previous two days—the anger that had made me want to expose Tomoko and Kurota's treachery for all the world to see when I found them. My interest in the matter had vanished and I could only wonder why had I chased such a man and woman to such a place. In the dim light I quickly wrote a telegram to Tsuyuko, since I could no longer return to Tokyo once I had found Tomoko and Kurota.

TRAVELING ON URGENT BUSINESS. CANNOT RETURN TOMORROW.
PLEASE FORGIVE ME.

The train stopped next at Suma and I planned to send the telegram from there. Where had this cool attitude of mine come from? Perhaps it wasn't coolness but rather the pride that remains to the end in the heart of a man confronting such a situation. Soon the conductor called out "Suma" several times and the train came to a stop. I jumped off, quickly walking several steps toward the station. But once there my body began to quake with a fierce revival of the longing I had experienced before getting on the train—I wanted to go back to Tokyo and meet Tsuyuko. Yes, I'll go back! Best to leave Tomoko to her mother anyway, I thought, coming to that decision on the spot. I quickly erased the message to Tsuyuko, turned the telegram over, and scribbled.

TOMOKO IS RIDING ON THIS TRAIN. PLEASE DO EVERYTHING
YOU CAN.

I folded the telegram several times and ran along the platform, searching for the mother's window. The train stopped at Suma for only a minute or two and had already begun to move when I finally found her staring out her window with an abstracted expression on her face.

"Please read this," I called to her.

"What is it?" I remember that she took out eyeglasses wrapped in cloth from the small bag on her lap.

119

The lights from the train windows shone upon the dark platform for a brief instant before the train disappeared. The steam whistle receded into the distance, leaving behind the quietly lapping sound of waves from a sea that seemed close enough to touch. Alone in the small dark station, I was barely able to believe the reason I was standing there. When I checked my watch I saw that there wasn't time to wait for a train to connect me to the last train leaving that night from Kobe to Tokyo. I got a taxi in front of the station and raced through the evening streets as if fleeing from something in hot pursuit.

.   .   .

At Kobe I got on the train that was going to Tokyo and slept like a dead man after the exhaustion of the last few days. Much later, Tomoko's mother told me about what had happened next. After she and I parted, the mother apparently sat there stunned. For a long time her mind had wandered off into a vast distance. She never wondered why I had written a message on that piece of paper instead of speaking to her, for the mere thought that her daughter was alive and, beyond all her expectations, riding in the same train set her emotions afire. The mother simply reviewed what she should say when they met and finally decided to discuss this with me. She waited for my return since she had absolutely no idea that I had left the train at Suma Station and would not come back. She waited, certain that I would come along any minute, but then too much time passed and she started thinking that maybe I was drinking in the dining car or already talking to Tomoko in one of the cars. At this she got very worried and decided to search the train on her own. She went to the dining car without finding me or Tomoko, and looked in the other cars but there too had no success. She returned once again to the dining car, where she had missed them before, but now saw Tomoko and Kurota sitting in a seat at the other end of the car, whispering to each other. Astonished, the mother did just as I had done before and hid behind the galley, keeping very still as she waited. In a moment Kurota got up and walked past the mother without noticing her. Tomoko, who followed behind, was about to go by when she stopped short in shock.

"Tomoko!"

"Don't say anything," Tomoko warned, her eyes quickly over-flowing with tears. "I'll be right back. Just wait here." She spoke quietly and rushed past the mother to follow Kurota.

The mother had just stood there, transfixed, and whether from happiness or grief—she herself did not know—tears streamed down her face. She might have imagined it but her daughter's appearance was unspeakably pathetic, for she had become painfully thin. And Tomoko's face had turned as white as paper when she saw her mother.

In a moment Tomoko returned, breathing nervously as she pulled at her mother's sleeve to lead her into the coffee shop. "I don't want to talk about it. Please, Mama, have pity on me and just be quiet. If he finds out that you're here, I don't know what I'll do."

"But, Tomoko, you're going to come home with me now, aren't you? We'll get off at the next stop and change trains."

"Everything's all right, Mama. I'm planning to come home soon. I just have to go to Hiroshima for a little while. I absolutely have to go there."

"I don't know how you can continue talking like this. Think about what Jōji is going through. You don't know how worried he is. He didn't sleep, running all over searching for you. Why, he's the one who found you for me just now."

Tomoko, who hadn't even dreamed that I had come along, turned pale at these words and clung to her mother, begging her to make absolutely sure that she didn't meet me. She had the idea that I'd kill her if we met. Only then did it finally occur to the mother that she really didn't know what had happened to me, since I hadn't shown up yet. She took out the piece of paper once again to show Tomoko.

"Where did he give this to you?" Tomoko asked.

The mother said she believed it had been at Suma. Then, the relief flowing into her face, Tomoko asserted that this certainly meant I had left the train there. Surely my writing "Please do everything you can" announced my intention to pull myself out of the matter and asked her to settle everything as best she could. If that were not the case, why would I have written the note and passed it to her? At this, the mother grasped the real circumstances and saw that the explanation made sense. However, she continued to insist that I'd been most inexcusably treated. "Just think how angry he must have been to have seen you and then bolt from the train." She kept repeating, "It's a disgrace, I tell you, a disgrace."

Tomoko had just listened to these complaints at first but finally gave her version of the story. She disclosed that I had been seeing a girlfriend named Tsuyuko since well before my marriage. In Tomoko's view I couldn't be bothered to waste an iota of sentiment on my former wife, Matsuyo, whereas Tsuyuko was always on my mind. After our marriage Tomoko would observe my behavior and, although I didn't say anything directly, she saw that Tsuyuko consumed my waking hours. A week after our marriage, she claimed, life in the house had become intolerably boring. Since Tomoko did not have the resources to find her own way of this trouble, she considered whom she could confide in and settled upon Kurota, her close friend from before the marriage. She didn't look on Kurota as someone she loved, but she needed a very close friend who would accompany her for walks down the streets, to drink coffee or see movies. So whatever she might have said, in her heart she never dreamed of eloping with Kurota. It was just that she eventually couldn't bear to wait silently by while I persisted in my obsession with Tsuyuko.

She was of course referring to the telegram Tsuyuko had sent to summon me, which arrived the day before she left the house. In fulfillment of Tomoko's every anticipation, I read the message and then rushed off to meet Tsuyuko the following morning. Tomoko believed that she knew—so surely she could almost sense it in her fingertips—just how I'd feel after seeing Tsuyuko. Perhaps I would not come back at all, or even if I did come back, my life with Tomoko would essentially be over. If that were the case, Tomoko would be abandoned. Since she would have preferred to die before permitting that to happen, she made up her mind on the spot to leave the house first and talked Kurota into joining her. The mother couldn't tell what part of Tomoko's story was a true expression of her feelings and what part a fabrication of the facts, but upon hearing the story for the first time she pitied her daughter for having gone through such an ordeal. The mother planned to meet with Kurota and try to straighten out the situation, even if they decided to go right back home afterwards.

Tomoko, however, absolutely refused to consider this. "You can't do that. He's terrified already. Talking to you would be too much for him. I can't tell him that you've come."

"Then I'll just wait for you here. You get your things together and tell Kurota-san what we've decided."

"Are you forcing me to go back, Mama?" Tomoko asked, full of resentment.

Here she had described the situation to her mother in great detail and if after all that effort she was still going to be forced to return home, then she wouldn't hesitate, she said, to throw herself from the window right in front of her mother's eyes. With tears streaming down her face, Tomoko bitterly criticized her mother for always interpreting everything she did as simple willfulness. The mother, naturally taken aback by this outburst, couldn't press her daughter further. Although the chances were that Tomoko only spoke for effect, the mother had no desire for more of a commotion than she already had on her hands. So in the end the mother had to give up trying to take her daughter back to Tokyo with her. Tomoko had to go to Hiroshima to settle her problems and her mother was to wait until then. The mother was instructed to be one of the last to get off the train at Hiroshima, to go out the gate and then entertain herself until one other train passed by. Only at that time was the mother to go to Kurota's house, saying that she had come to pick up Tomoko. Perhaps by that time, they would have come to an agreement. Tomoko wrote the address, Kurota Hospital, 7 chōme, Ōtemachi, on a piece of paper and gave it to her mother. Then Tomoko returned to where Kurota was sitting.

Of course the mother's anxiety about her daughter's behavior increased when she found herself alone again, for what if Tomoko had just used those words as a ruse and actually planned to drop out of sight once she had the chance? The mother sat there, uneasy and forlorn, but Tomoko found opportunities to leave Kurota and come over for quiet chats, also bringing over some food, much to her mother's relief. Soon after daybreak the train arrived in Hiroshima, where the mother delayed her exit and was the last to go out the gate. She saw her daughter and Kurota off in the distance, their arms locked in a most friendly fashion as they walked. The mother relaxed, took a bath, and had tea at a stall in front of the station which served as a rest area. When the next outbound train came in, she took a taxi to the Kurota house. The house, which turned out to be quite a distance from the railroad, was located on a quiet residential street and connected to a large hospital next door. When the maid came out, the mother explained the reason for her visit and at this an uproar billowed through the house. The mother was led into a dim tatami room facing the courtyard. This sturdy house was typical of the residences of old country families, but surprisingly the whole atmosphere further discouraged the mother. In a moment a small old woman, who was apparently the mother of the house, came out and polite introductions were exchanged. Kurota's mother went on to declare formally that what her son had done was unforgivable and she apologized, obviously wracked by remorse. Although Kurota's mother spoke in the simple style of the countryside, a parent's overwhelming grief was expressed in her every word and gesture. Tomoko's mother was startled to find herself on the verge of tears as she protested that in fact her own daughter's indiscretions were responsible for the turmoil.

Tomoko's mother didn't know what to say since she had no information about what her daughter and Kurota had made public since their arrival. Prudence required that she not say anything that would cause trouble. Soon Kurota's father came in, also making profuse apologies and saying that he deeply regretted his son's reprehensible behavior. He went on to declare that he would do all he could to make amends. From what he said, Tomoko's mother managed to gather that Tomoko was pregnant. Tomoko had conceived this child, hidden the fact from her parents, then married me. Recently I had caught wind of the pregnancy and as a result of the ensuing furor the two of them had fled to Hiroshima. Since they couldn't return to Tokyo, the father asked that they be allowed to get married.

Tomoko's mother listened to the father's words but could not immediately decide what was the truth and what mere melodrama. This was the first she'd heard of Tomoko's pregnancy and naturally she had to collect herself somewhat before she could proceed. Since she also didn't know how to take his assertion that he would definitely make amends for what had happened, the mother decided to consult with her daughter to find out the details. She asked to see Tomoko. Soon after the parents departed, there was the clattering of Tomoko's short, quick steps as she rushed down the hall.

"It's all right, Mama." She smiled shyly as she plopped herself down next to her mother.

"Are you really pregnant?"

"It's all right. It's not Kurota's. I had to say that or else they wouldn't have let me into the house. Afterwards, when we're on the train, I'll tell you all about it. Hurry and get ready. I feel so miserable here."

The mother was astounded as she studied her daughter's face. "Have you settled everything?"

"Talking to them doesn't accomplish anything. They're all so stubborn I can't stand it."

"Yes, but what about Kurota-san?"

"I can't depend on him." She sounded very unhappy. "He just gets confused and then he's absolutely worthless to me. Oh please, let's go."

The mother heard her daughter's brisk explanation but of course had great difficulty taking her seriously, for almost as soon as she had arrived Tomoko was announcing that they should leave. This change of heart the mother did not attribute to her daughter's usual willfulness, but instead she pitied Tomoko, who, she sensed, had found the actual atmosphere of the house completely, unexpectedly different from what she had imagined it would be. Whatever the reason, the mother was delighted that Tomoko wished to return home. She told Tomoko to get ready, calculating that if they left quickly they might be able to catch the earliest afternoon train back to Tokyo. The mother again spoke to Kurota's parents, who both seemed afraid to state their opinions, not out of reserve but because they hoped to minimize the effects of this calamity upon themselves.

Tomoko's mother couldn't decide what she should say and vaguely surmised that while they intended to take the major responsibility for Tomoko's pregnancy and elopement, this did not necessarily mean that they wanted the marriage to take place. In fact, they just wished to cause as little damage to Kurota and Tomoko as possible. Kurota's mother, however, could hardly contain her sadness when it was decided that Tomoko would go back with her mother. She urged them to delay their departure to the later train, for after all Tomoko and Kurota had fled all the way to Hiroshima together and she wanted them to at least have the time to say their farewells. Yet the father, his face proclaiming that this was out of the question, maintained that henceforth the parents on both sides should be left to settle everything and was absolutely opposed to having those two meet again, since they had acted so improperly. Besides, their son had already been sent to his uncle's house.

"That's enough, Mama." Tomoko knit her brow in consternation since she couldn't bear to stay in that depressing house a moment longer.

They hastily excused themselves and at last departed. Later the mother conceded that she might have been just an indulgent parent, but her own sorrow was so intense that she didn't know what to say as she gazed at her daughter walking away with her face buried in her coat collar. "Let's send a telegram to Papa right away," the mother suggested, but Tomoko didn't answer. The mother did send a telegram to her husband in Tokyo, then bought the tickets and put Tomoko on the train. But just as the train was about to leave, Kurota appeared running breathlessly along the platform. When Tomoko saw him chasing beside the departing train and bawling messages to her, even she started to cry. Soon Kurota faded from view.

Relief surged through the mother's heart, for if they could just get back to Tokyo she felt that somehow the nightmare would end. It was her private wish merely to bring Tomoko safely back to her father. However, even while she was so overwrought, she could not help wondering about me and what exactly had happened after I had left the train at Suma. Of course she couldn't think of having Tomoko return to me in the wake of this commotion, but the mother even repeated to me afterwards that this is what she actually wished. Whether I had a lover named Tsuyuko or not, the mother still wanted me as Tomoko's husband, for she believed that I was a hundred times more dependable than that child Kurota. Anyway, the train carrying the mother and daughter went from Hiroshima to Kobe, then Osaka, and at Nagoya visitors came into their car in the middle of the night. When the mother recognized them as her husband's older sister and her husband, she was naturally puzzled about how those two relatives had come to know that she and Tomoko were on that train. They told her that they'd received a telegram with instructions to get the mother and Tomoko to leave the train at Nagoya. A separate telegram had come for Tomoko and her mother, saying only that the father would come from Tokyo to meet them and that they should rest for a day or two at the aunt's house. Details would follow in a letter. The mother could not understand why they had to get off the train midway, but since her sister-in-law and her husband didn't seem to know the actual story, the mother pretended that she and her daughter were on their way back from a sightseeing trip to Kyoto and Osaka. It seemed wise to get off the train but in her alarm over what must have been happening in Tokyo the mother found herself brooding over the dire possibilities. Maybe another crisis had developed or perhaps I had frightened her husband with yet another piece of news? Mystified, the two went along to spend the night with the aunt and uncle. The next day a thick special delivery letter arrived from the father. What he had written came as a complete surprise to her, and even now when I remember how the mother looked when she described the contents, an odd feeling, at once cold and dull, overpowers me.

> Today Jōji came to the house and had a small surgical scalpel wrapped in cloth hidden in his coat pocket. I am probably mistaken about this, but just to be on the safe side, keep Tomoko there for the time being. After I know in detail what Jōji's plans really are, I'll go there to pick you up myself. I urge you to consider this matter very seriously.

The father had written out of extreme anxiety, as if I had become completely deranged by Tomoko's misbehavior and wanted to cause her physical harm. But frankly I had other matters on my mind, issues that had nothing at all to do with Tomoko.

. . .

From the moment I'd caught sight of Tomoko and Kurota in Kobe, I completely lost interest in them as if the spirit that had possessed me lost its hold on my soul. Also the fierceness I had felt, my vow to search heaven and earth for them—all this had disappeared without a trace and I became inordinately sleepy, dozing like a dead man until my arrival at Shimbashi Station the next morning. When I checked my watch I saw that it was three minutes before eleven— even the train seemed to have been scheduled to accommodate my meeting with Tsuyuko. I would describe my mood at that moment as light and cheerful, and I went to the clothing store outside the station and bought some new handkerchiefs among other things. I waited in front of the staircase of the Tōyōken where we always met but Tsuyuko didn't appear. Since she was rarely even two minutes late for an appointment, I began to fear that once again a calamity had struck.

Then an old woman came quietly walking over to me. She had been sitting in a chair near the entrance to the women's waiting room, visible from where I was, and looking my way for some time. "It's Yuasa-san, isn't it? I thought so but . . ."

She wore a black velvet shawl and I immediately remembered her face with its friendly smile from the morning after the night Tsuyuko and I had stayed at the apartment of Oyae from the Yūyūtei. I had briefly met this old woman when I had taken Tsuyuko home to her Yotsuya house, and actually I had thought of her face a great deal, eagerly anticipating the day when she would have something to tell me, especially since Tsuyuko had mentioned that she was our only ally.

"I came today with a message from the young lady."

"Tsuyuko can't come, is that it?"

"No, she . . ."

The old woman had been asked to tell me that some relatives had arrived in the morning and Tsuyuko would not be able to get away by eleven. Since she felt we couldn't talk there, she suggested tea and we went upstairs together to the Tōyōken, where I received some surprising advice from her.

"You know," she began, "I look at what you both are doing and sometimes I get very irritated. When I see this go on and on, I wonder what you plan to do. Sometimes I wonder whether you're really serious. You've started something but you don't seem able to finish it. Isn't it like only partially killing a snake? If you want to put an end to it, then why don't you do it once and for all? Or if you plan to continue, isn't there something else you can do?"

"Something else I can do?"

"Why not run away with the young lady? Why couldn't you just go to Osaka or to Kobe or Sapporo? It's not as if you have to live in Tokyo. Go and live somewhere together. See how things work out and then you can come back here."

I didn't reply, not because I questioned her motives but because it struck me as odd that here was someone still trying to work up the desire in me to do something. I had slept soundly and felt unexpectedly well after the confusion of the past two or three days, but deep within me I could still hear Matsuyo, who had smiled so scornfully: *Even now, with the rope practically around your neck, you can't get rid of your vanity, can you? You must be joking, thinking that Tomoko is going to kill herself because of you.* Or Momoko's laughter: *Really, Yuasa-san, don't you see that the hospital she was going to was Kurota?* The image of Kurota and Tomoko together on the train surfaced in my mind. What actually was the point of continuing in such a world? A feeling of dark revulsion for life on this earth overcame me, and I wondered if I would ever rid myself of the self-disgust that made me want to vomit. It was no wonder the old woman's words were unsettling.

"Why don't you say something? Perhaps it's rude of me to talk like this, but you know, you're the one who is completely responsible for the young lady's present state. Don't you feel any pity for her? Why can't you be decisive and make some clear plans for her? She's wasting her time just waiting. I wonder what you're waiting for." She hesitated for a moment before gazing at me briefly. "And believe me, waiting won't accomplish anything. Do you know what

Tsuyuko's father thinks of you? He says you're absolutely crazy. What is the sense of having anything to do with a man who is crazy, he says."

I could hear Tsuyuko's father saying those words, but oddly enough no antagonism for him followed. Actually, I was so tired by then that I felt like wearily agreeing when I heard his opinion of me. In a sense, calling me crazy seemed perfectly understandable, but then too I still burned with hostility for the atmosphere in Tsuyuko's house that had nurtured such attitudes.

"Thank you for your concern. But has Tsuyuko spoken to you about any of this?"

"No," the woman strongly protested. "She knows nothing about it. She'll come here this afternoon at one o'clock. Take her and go away somewhere, even today. I'll manage things for you here."

I listened to the old woman and then we parted. It was my firm belief that even if we did try to elope, no purpose would be served, and if this was my attitude I supposed that Tsuyuko had even stronger convictions in that regard. But what should we do, I wondered. How was I to resolve such a complicated situation so that I could return to a normal relationship with Tsuyuko? The old woman had no idea what course we should follow, but had merely voiced the meddlesome thoughts she'd been rehashing inside her cheerless room in the Yotsuya house. Without knowing about Tomoko or Matsuyo or even the feelings of Tsuyuko herself, she had just said whatever was on her mind, droning on like a sightseer in need of diversion. That was my attitude as I walked along the street alone. I had come as far as I could and found a wall in front of me, with no place to turn. Should I turn around or should I just go crashing into that wall?

When I thought of how I had possessed at least some will when I saw Tsuyuko three days before and how I now felt thoroughly exhausted, it was like the difference between night and day. If Tsuyuko came that afternoon still feeling as she had before, that she had no strength to go on, then I believed I too might be drowned in her immense fatigue. Lacking the strength to pull Tsuyuko back to the real world of the living, I was overcome with a kind of dizziness, like the queasiness of a drunkard who just wants to be dragged unsteadily along. This was not despair I was giving in to, but a more active pull, perhaps toward decadence. For I had changed since the other day and had now wrenched myself free of ordinary restraints. My body could easily move in any direction, like a speck of matter in the depths of the deepest sea. In a world where such fine things as laws and morality and promises between people seemed impossibly distant, I could do anything! I might have been fearful of what was to come but still I throbbed with a certain ecstasy. In this world beyond society's rules, Tsuyuko was definitely mine! Perhaps that day, for the first time, I would be able to bind her body together with mine. Such ideas preoccupied me during the two hours that I waited for her.

I decided to stop at my house in Ōmori and the maid greeted me with a worried expression.

"No one has come?" I asked.

"No. No one has been here."

The house was in perfect order, left just as it was when Tomoko had been there, and I drank the hot tea Tsune brought for me, soothing her apprehensions with the news that I had located Tomoko.

"I see." She lifted her dull eyes and then looked down again.

"I'm going to go out again, but I'll be right back."

I returned to Shimbashi Station and Tsuyuko soon appeared at the ticket gate as expected, in the same blue coat she had worn the last time. "Excuse me for being late," she apologized.

"Would it be all right if we went to my house today? We can relax there."

"To your house?" Tsuyuko was having difficulty absorbing my abrupt suggestion.

"Tomoko has left, so you can come over without causing any problems."

Tsuyuko remained silent and then turned to me, quietly asking, "What happened?"

"We've separated. As long as you're in Japan, I can't possibly live with her."

"But . . ." Once again Tsuyuko searched my face. "Can you get married and separated as easily as that? It upsets me to think that you separated because of me."

"You weren't the cause, it happened naturally. But will it bother you too much to go to my house?"

"It won't bother me but . . ." Tsuyuko smiled with an inexplicable sweetness.

The plan previously laid out by the servant made little sense as far as I was concerned, but Tsuyuko so touched my heart with her gentle manner that I wondered whether I could carry out the old woman's scheme had I the desire. Once at the house I took Tsuyuko to the room in the back which had been Tomoko's. Since only one small window faced the garden it was the best place for avoiding curious eyes. But Tsuyuko just stood there, apparently uncomfortable, and looked around the room.

"Won't you take off your coat?"

Tsuyuko removed her blue coat as if peeling away her skin and her ears strained to identify the sounds around her. But soon her expression altered to a playful smile as she pointed to Tomoko's red slippers near the stove. "Look at those!"

"You can try them on if you like."

The laugh that came to Tsuyuko's lips expressed her surprise at the stove which burned warmly, the red rug with the pillows strewn about, and the piano—evidence of my domestic life which she had never seen before.

"Strange," she said.

"Why is that?"

"When I am here like this, I feel as if I have become your wife."

"That's what your old servant suggested. She said that I shouldn't let you go home today. She wanted me to shut you up in this house. What do you think? It isn't out of the question if it's what you want."

"Oh, she really is impossible." Tsuyuko stood up to open the piano cover and idly struck several keys. Soon she was playing restlessly in a high octave. I lit a cigarette and as if in a dream gazed at Tsuyuko's narrow shoulders swaying to the music. Of course what I had talked of before had been presented lightly, but I returned to the thought: if Tsuyuko and I so wished, she could live in this room which had been Tomoko's only two days previously. This could be arranged quite naturally. Nothing was impossible. Although I had not intended it, the situation had developed on its own and what could possibly be wrong with Tsuyuko's remaining there from that day on? Consumed by this fantasy I was amused to think that we could defy fate. Yes, we'll go ahead and do it! Then for no particular reason I drew back the window curtain and saw the dog Tomi sitting in front of the porch, its head oddly angled, barking as it always did at the sound of the piano or the phonograph. Tomoko had brought Tomi along from the house in Senzoku. In fact, the piano Tsuyuko was playing, the sofa, the display shelves—these had all been brought there by Tomoko. If the trouble with Tomoko were resolved and her possessions removed from the house, what would remain of the stage props in this play? Every trace of the house's coziness would be gone and once again I'd be left to mope about among the scrap piles of a student of painting. It struck me as ludicrous that even the fantasy I'd just fabricated could be at the mercy of this insignificant piano and red rug.

"Excuse me, sir." Tsune's voice sounded restrained as she called to me from the other side of the door. Then she softly announced, "Takahashi-san has come to see you."

At the mere mention of Takahashi, Matsuyo's family name, I felt as if I'd been doused with cold water. Much subdued, I followed Tsune out to the back door to find Matsuyo standing there in a blazing red coat I hadn't seen before. She was wearing so much eye makeup that even from a distance I could see every detail.

She laughed at me as a greeting. "When did you come back?"

"Where would I be coming back from? And why are you here now?"

"Did you see Tomoko? Don't try to hide anything from me. I know all about it. You went to Kobe with Tomoko's mother, didn't you?"

When I looked at her smiling face mocking me, the memory of how angry I'd been several nights before once again boiled up within my chest. I couldn't quiet the impulse that made me want to deposit a good hard blow on those thin, smirking lips of hers. Now that Tomoko had left me, Matsuyo plainly intended to get a look at the beaten expression on my face.

"Tell me," I said, "if you know everything, why do you bother to ask? You know, you really are a fool. If you're not careful, I'll hit you. You'd better leave fast if you don't want to get hurt."

"Quite the bully, aren't you?" Matsuyo moved back a bit, still with that mocking smile on her face. "You know, Okano told me that if you still don't have any clear plan for helping me, he'll disclose everything in the newspaper. It'll be a full expose of Yuasa Jōji and he'll make sure that all decent citizens here denounce you."

"You ass!" Without thinking, I lunged at Matsuyo but she was already out the door.

"What do I care if you go crying afterwards?" Matsuyo sneered as her parting shot. "The very day after Tomoko leaves, you drag in your old girlfriend. You really are a complete louse, aren't you?"

Once her words were out, the door was fanned by the wind and sprang shut. I realized that Matsuyo had heard the piano which Tsuyuko had continued to play as if unaware of the argument outside. Out of breath, I stood there for some time and saw Okano's red face as he had sat drinking by the brazier at Matsuyo's house that night. Matsuyo had been too stupid to see that she should have kept the intimacy of their relationship a secret. And this same Okano, she had declared, would expose everything in the newspapers. Even though I hardly cared about what happened to me, my anger had nearly gone out of control. It was clear to me that Matsuyo's intent was not so much obtaining money as getting me to rot to my very core. The way Matsuyo saw the situation, I had always fallen right into her trap and that of course also galled me. I went down to the bathroom and washed my hands, lost in thought. I waited for a bit before returning to Tsuyuko. Still playing the piano, she didn't seem to realize that I'd returned.

"Would you like something to drink?" I took a bottle of wine from the shelf and poured some into glasses.

Tsuyuko was silent as she brought the wine to her mouth, merely wetting her lips before she put the glass down.

"Did you think over what I said to you?"

"I didn't have to think about it further. If you knew the truth you'd be surprised. I should tell you that all this came about very naturally. You told me before that you'd be unhappy if it were your fault that Tomoko and I separated. But tell me, how would you feel if it weren't your fault?"

"Even if it is my fault, I don't care." Tsuyuko spoke with a smile while her eyes conveyed other meanings. "My reaction would be the same whether Tomoko were here or not. I think that's reasonable, don't you? You know, I haven't spent a single day doubting your love for me. Whether you're still married or not, it doesn't matter at all. Do you see what I mean?"

"Are you saying you don't want to think about my actual situation? Is it because you don't want to become my wife? Tell me, Tsuyuko." I spoke her name quite naturally and a light, clear sensation—almost a feeling of ease—filled my soul. "You know, you've probably been reading too many fairy tales. Isn't it true? If you really want us to live together, you have to forget those fairy tales. And let me tell you, you are my wife whether you like the idea or not. Today I won't let you go home, no matter what you say. You'll stay here and if anyone objects, well, I'm ready for them."

The image of Matsuyo's face alone was enough to make me vow to fight them all if necessary. A sudden conviction that it would all be easy moved me to embrace Tsuyuko, and we kissed for a long time while outside the quiet deepened like a darkening hillside. When the cuckoo clock above us slowly sang out five o'clock, I vaguely recalled that the clock also belonged to Tomoko and with that thought, unspeakable images of an empty, senseless life came crowding back to me. It's just pictures in the sand you're painting, I told myself, and when that conclusion flitted across my consciousness and reached Tsuyuko, she started sobbing on my chest. "It's all hopeless . . . hopeless!" She cried fiercely, writhing like a child. Bewildered by her outburst, I embraced Tsuyuko all the more as if to compel a fresh power to surge up within me.

"What are you calling hopeless? Don't worry about anything. It'll be fine." I did not know myself what I meant by this.

Though much time passed, Tsuyuko would not stop her crying

and later I understood that she must have known of Matsuyo's visit. She insisted that she didn't care about Tomoko or even Matsuyo but she couldn't have said otherwise when thrust into that complicated situation. It was natural that a young woman who had just turned twenty would feel bewildered. I struggled to control my own confusion as I felt Tsuyuko's shoulders shaking with grief in the gathering darkness. Tsune must have been reluctant to come in and turn on the lights since she had not looked in even once. Still embracing Tsuyuko, I brought her quietly to the bed in the cool adjoining room as pale moonlight shone through the thin curtains. "Tsuyuko," I called out to her softly. She had closed her eyes and her eyelids, swollen from crying, were like two pink sea shells on a pale beach. Now and then she drew in a breath and each time her lips trembled, wrenching my heart. Dying together with Tsuyuko would be perfectly natural—not because we could not live, but because dying was the most natural step for us to take. Of course those perceptions weren't so clear as yet, but intimations of life's emptiness had seeped into my soul as I held Tsuyuko's chilled body in my arms.

"Excuse me, sir." Tsune was outside the door, her words barely audible.

"I'm coming." I put on my slippers and emerged from the room.

She had made dinner and asked if we would eat. When I saw how worried Tsune was, I spoke as if coming out of a trance and said that her meal wasn't needed since we planned to go to a restaurant.

By the time I returned, Tsuyuko had opened her eyes wide in the darkness. "I have to go home."

"You're going to go home? Are you really, after all?"

"Yes. I have some things to settle before I come back. The next time I come, I won't go back. You get ready too."

She perhaps meant that I too should make preparations for dying, but as she spoke she combed her disheveled hair and smiled quietly. It was past seven by my watch and I thought that I would see Tsuyuko safely home and then begin to settle my affairs. When I left the house with Tsuyuko I was in a calm frame of mind, as if I were accompanying a member of the family who was going out on a brief errand and would soon return.

. . .

After leaving Tsuyuko I went to Hongo to settle some business. On the way back I came out on the street in front of the ward office and saw a large sign announcing a going-out-of-business sale at a medical supply store. I wandered around the store for a bit, studying the surgical tables and pieces of medical equipment. The displays glittered in electric lighting as bright as the noonday sun. While my eyes scanned dozens of surgical scissors and scalpels lined up in a glass cabinet on one side, a whole scene from my past came back to me, a time about thirteen years before when a friend of mine became absolutely fed up with life because of family problems and actually killed himself by cutting his carotid artery. His whole drama returned with a vividness that made it seem like only yesterday.

There may be people who remember the old Ginza group of those days called Zanboa, whose members—literary people and artists associated with Kitahara Hakushū—used to exhibit their works around town. A young friend of mine, the proprietor of the florist shop Kenchi-ya, was so impressed by the group that he formed his own circle of literary people and artists to pursue similar activities. Night after night they'd have stalls at Yotsuya devoted to their pursuits. Late one night, this Kenchi-ya proprietor sat with his friends in the shop and we became engrossed in a discussion of the most efficient way to commit suicide. Fools that we were, we talked about how drowning involved more agony than was really needed, and that hanging was easier but afterwards you would leave an ugly mess too embarrassing for all concerned. Then this proprietor of Kenchi-ya announced that he had an excellent device to show us. He pulled out a desk drawer and opened a home medical equipment kit. One of the scalpels served for his demonstration when he angled it downwards, slicing as if he were cutting his neck. "All you have to do is drink a lot of liquor—then, just when the circulation of the blood has really churned up, you thrust it in hard. That's the easiest way, I've decided." He talked seriously of such deadly matters but this kind of conversation had already become standard with him and he was forever telling us about how he was going to kill himself. We'd become used to his speeches and so we just brushed this one off as more of the usual. His wife, whom he had supposedly married for love, had found herself some new young man. The Kenchi-ya proprietor himself had also become intimate with the young woman from the sandal shop across the way and so his house was in a constant state of war, but no one really believed that he would actually kill himself.

However, when it was still dark the next morning, someone knocked on my rear storm window to wake me. The proprietor of Kenchi-ya had died and I was told to go over to his house right away. Once there I was shocked to find the room filled with flowers from his shop, which had been scattered all over. He had collapsed on the large organ in the corner, apparently dead. The scene was just what he had described the night before—an empty bottle of cognac lay overturned beside him and the blood splashed all over the walls and on the ceiling looked as if it had been sprayed. An absolutely gruesome sight—the blood had spread farther than seemed physically possible. That room was very much on my mind as I stood looking at the scalpels lined up in the glass cabinet of the medical equipment store. No sooner had I remembered the episode than I wished to buy one of those scalpels for myself. The young clerk carefully wrapped the scalpel in cotton and placed it in a box, and I casually put this in my coat pocket before going out to the street. I had purchased the scalpel for no particular purpose and had no intention of bringing harm to myself or trying to end my life by my own hand.

I remember the night as cold and freezing, without any wind. My mood was oddly bright on the way home as if I'd made a major decision. But then, remembering that I had to tell Tomoko's father about what had happened during the trip to Kobe, I went over to their house in Senzoku. When the father saw me, he was a bit surprised.

"Well, hello." Flustered, he did not meet my eyes. "You certainly have had a hard time." I told him in detail what had happened, how we'd searched at different hotels in Kobe and then, fearing that we wouldn't be able to find Tomoko and Kurota, had taken the train to Shimonoseki, and how I'd been surprised to spot them from the rear in one of the cars. I also told him how I'd believed that if I met them face to face, I might lose control of myself and make a difficult situation even more intolerable. So I'd left everything to her mother, got off the train at Suma, and had come back to Tokyo. It was no surprise that the father heaved a sigh of relief, and thanked me for my efforts.

He kept saying how good it was that I'd come to see things in that light. "I completely understand how you must feel. I thank you. After this, won't you please trust in me and leave it to me to settle matters for the time being? I definitely will make it up to you."

He repeated these apologies but I was already far removed from the flagrant humiliation Tomoko had forced me to endure until two days previously. In fact, I had a certain magnanimous sense that I was responsible for the way things had turned out and so I felt guilty about just sitting and listening to him talk. On the other hand, I didn't want to tell him about Tsuyuko, so I remained silent, stifling my desire to say that it was really nothing, that in fact I felt relieved of a burden and very lighthearted. As I sat across from Tomoko's father, my heart expanded with a deeply human warmth for a close relative, an emotion I hadn't experienced for a long time. I knew I probably wouldn't be able to see the father again and this made me feel lonelier than did the end of my marriage to Tomoko. Just then the maid came in to say that the bath was ready.

"Bath?" The father indicated that this was hardly the time for a bath, but then he looked over at me. "What about you? You must be tired after the train ride. How about a bath?"

Once the question was put to me, I realized that I'd been so busy that I hadn't had a bath that morning. "Yes, if you don't mind, I think I will," I replied, and went off to the bath.

I put some effort into washing off the several days' accumulation of dirt and grime from my trip and I was feeling marvelously relaxed as I dried myself. When I finished the maid called out from the other side of the translucent glass door, "The master is waiting for you in the study."

Carefree after my bath, I followed her to a room that was less a study than a formal Western-style receiving room on the second floor. There the father waited with a portentous expression on his face, a completely different person from before. A large table was between us and he faced me directly from the other side, but as soon as I sat down he took out a small white object from his pocket and placed it on the table. He brought one clenched fist to his eye and then—just as they describe a man grieving—his voice rose in a sharp, choking cry and he began to sob. What he had set on the table was the scalpel I had just bought in Hongo. I had put the box in my coat pocket but the father must have caught sight of it while I was in the bath, for the scalpel had been taken out from the box and lay there still wrapped in white cotton. I was rendered speechless by this unexpected turn of events and unsure about what I was expected to do next.

"Jōji, I wonder if I could ask you to tell me what you plan to do with this scalpel. I didn't believe that you—" he started to say, and again there were those choking sobs in his throat.

Perhaps I should have told him honestly about how I'd felt when I bought the scalpel, omitting mention of Tsuyuko, but I was so taken aback that I was unable to get myself to do even this.

"I didn't realize that things had upset you this much, Jōji," he continued in the same tone. "Do you think that since I've offered you my apologies about Tomoko you might reconsider your plans? I would never dream of allowing you to be disgraced by this. I don't know how you feel, but when you married Tomoko I really thought of you as my son. I always believed I would help you—as much as my poor endeavors would allow—not only with your marriage but with your work and with your future so that you could succeed, just as I would do for my own son. Tomoko's imprudent behavior has brought us to this unhappy end, but be that as it may, my previous feelings have not changed. If you will agree, I would like us to be a real father and son from now on and into the future. What do you think about this, Jōji? Won't you do that for me? Please let me take care of your future as part of my obligation as your father. I intend to set you up in the world. It's natural that you feel as if there's no way out for you. That's natural. Please, I ask you, out of consideration for me, to have patience. I would like you to entrust your future, as well as this scalpel, to me."

I listened without saying a word and at last understood his meaning. He was under the impression that I was going to use the scalpel to harm Tomoko or even kill Tomoko and then die with her. He had in fact become extremely fearful once he started to consider what violence might result. At the same time, he did pity me for being so at my wit's end. He seemed willing to risk his own life so that I might be pulled back from the brink and brought out into the light. I tried to laugh away the father's worries, but even I sensed the awkwardness of my effort.

"It's all right, Father. Why worry about such foolishness? If I really had that in mind, do you think I would have left the train at Suma? Today I happened to pass a sale at a store that was going out of business and I bought the scalpel on a whim. Actually I plan to use it in painting my pictures."

"Is that true, Jōji?"

"Yes, of course. It's just coincidence that I bought the scalpel on my way over here. I don't like to see you so disturbed. Believe me, I won't do anything extreme, no matter what happens between Tomoko and me. So please, don't worry."

As I talked, tears flowed from my eyes like warm water. Strangely enough, at that moment I somehow got the crazy idea that I had really bought that scalpel to kill myself. It was also true that this good man had made me see into a sincere heart for the very first time. I cried, and the intensity of my emotion increased as I wept. It was many years since I had felt that way and while I cried the father spoke above my weeping.

"Well, then," he finally declared, "I'll take this scalpel. You stop your crying, Jōji."

I swallowed my tears at last and a cooling breeze blew across my heart. I saw that I hadn't intended to die after all, but in that moment dying seemed quite easy.

I talked with the father until late and when I left, sometime after one, a freezing mist covered the night. "It's cold. Put this on," the father urged, coming all the way out to the taxi with a blanket for my legs. I found out later that the father, exceedingly worried about my state of mind that night, then sent the telegram to his relatives in Nagoya instructing them to meet Tomoko and her mother, who were still on the Hiroshima train en route to Tokyo. You might say that the father had worried needlessly or you might say that he had cause. At that point even I was unsure about how I should conduct myself.

. . .

For several days I saw no one and stayed in the house. Although my state of mind was neither happy nor sad, I was never free of the peculiarly empty feeling that nothing in life was really worth doing. Why had I been rushing around to this country and that, busily working for so long? When living in Japan and for the entire seven years abroad, I had been like a man possessed, utterly consumed in my work. Granted, the sensation was vague and undefined, but it seemed that a force from behind had pushed my life in that direction. Had I ever had any clear aim in mind as I struggled? I had indeed, I told myself, recalling a time in the distant past. Years ago Matsuyo had followed me to Paris and eventually the child was born. The child was cute, smiling in his white hood, and I found him so appealing that I wouldn't have regretted working like a slave for that child. For my child, I would even have toiled at menial work or carried an aluminum lunch pail every day. A bright sense of purpose had filled that time. My love for the child didn't change after Matsuyo returned to Japan with him. But then there was the great earthquake in Japan, and in foreign countries, where the true facts were not known at first, it was reported that all of Japan had been reduced to ashes. When I contemplated the possibility that the child and Matsuyo were dead, I fell into a despair so profound that I became almost totally unhinged, as if I'd only been living for the two of them. If that frame of mind had continued, I would have become a doting parent just like every other father in the world with an intense commitment to living. I remembered those days.

But when I returned to Japan the child and Matsuyo had undergone such profound changes that they could have been different people. The child who had worn a white hood was then nine years old. He was sucking on cheap sweets and looked at me as I were some distant acquaintance. When the frightened child stared at me, his deep distrust was apparent.

"Kaname, say hello to Papa. Look at that face." Matsuyo laughed and cast a brief flirtatious glance at me.

What I saw were bleak eyes heavy with makeup. Until the night my ship arrived, Matsuyo had been working at a dance hall and her dance hall girl's manner remained even at the dock. My wife and my child. Of course I didn't have any right to criticize their unexpected transformation and I well knew that there had been few alternatives available while they waited for me. Yet my efforts to accept the change failed and I stopped loving them. I returned to the isolation I had endured while painting alone in my lodgings abroad and resumed hard work. Work. My work would be my salvation. At first this appeared to be a reasonable solution to my distress, but as I worked I realized that after so many years away my work had lost its intimate connections to Japanese society. Left behind by events, I could not find a new way to go about my work and great anxiety resulted. Japan had become more unknown to me than a foreign country. With nothing to rely on, I was continually tormented by a sense of isolation from the life around me. In the house I refused to talk and each time I sat down I sensed my body sinking into the floor. I feared that in time I would disappear altogether. I had sought Tsuyuko's love the way a baby searches for a mother's breast, but no matter how long I journeyed I still found no refuge where my heart could come to rest. It was as if I were walking in the dead of night along a windy street while the rest of the world basked in the warmth of their homes. Since I alone had to walk to the ends of the earth in that cold wind, I wondered if someone were forcing me into such a life or whether my nature had doomed me to this existence. Worse still, in resolving to end my life I simply might have been conforming to the schedule that had been prearranged for me long ago. It did seem that circumstances had somehow driven me to the point where I now found myself.

One morning Tsuyuko telephoned to say she was going to leave her house as soon as she was alone and wanted me to meet her at Shinano Station immediately. When I got there I found her standing under the eaves of a shop wearing a white shawl over her regular clothing.

"I can stay out for an hour. Shall we go to Gaien Park?" She continued to speak as we made our way there. "Today I went through all my letters and burned all of yours. In about three days I'll have everything settled. Tell me, is that all right with you?"

Tsuyuko by then believed that I too had become intent on dying and I didn't find anything extraordinary in what she was saying. On that cold morning, with faint sunlight passing through the sparse trees to the street, we were the only two out for a walk. Tsuyuko had worn white tabi and as I admired her feet moving slowly along, a freezing loneliness gripped me.

"It's all settled, isn't it?" she asked. "I'm still worried. I want to be sure you know that once I leave my house I refuse to go back. I absolutely refuse. That's going to be my attitude when I walk out. But I'm afraid that you'll change your mind. As for myself, I'm convinced there's no way we will be able to live together. Without you, I would have to die by myself and I don't want to die alone."

"Don't worry—it will be the greatest pleasure to die with you."

Some color rose into Tsuyuko's pale cheeks. "You have made up your mind then?"

I nodded, not saying anything. Tsuyuko was concerned about how we would take our lives, for she was determined to have a splendid end. She kept repeating that she didn't want to leave a wretched-looking corpse behind. At that moment, the scalpel that Tomoko's father had taken from me in the Senzoku house came floating up before my eyes. Yes, we would do it with that! With this decision, a chill of pleasure went up my spine. There was great joy in dying so easily and peacefully.

"The sixteenth then?" I asked as we stood in front of Sendagaya Station.

"Meet me at Shibuya at exactly ten in the morning."

Once Tsūyuko had disappeared beyond the ticket gate, I strode off without looking back.

With only three days remaining, I set aside a full day to organize my affairs at home, and while I was going about those tasks I essentially forgot that my work was preparation for ending my life. I mechanically disposed of one matter after another as if busy with a spring cleaning. Actually, my life had become so confused that if I'd intended to go on living I wouldn't have known what to do about those entanglements, but now that I had decided to die I went about settling my affairs with gusto. I became the superbly efficient committee member who found it easy to ignore the general state of bankruptcy. Afterwards I brought my desk up to the window of the study I had just cleaned out and began writing. I had no final words for anyone particular in mind, just a vague desire to leave a last testament. My pen scratched across the page in the quiet of the house as I recorded thoughts addressed to myself alone.

"You're feeling energetic, aren't you?" My landlord was working in the garden despite his age, and he called to me from outside. "Are you writing a novel?"

"Yes. A novel."

Two mornings later I went to visit several of my senior colleagues to offer my farewells. I took a couple of my paintings to the owner of the bookstore in Kōjimachi who was my one and only patron at the time. The previous day I had destroyed all the works in my studio I no longer cared for and the two I brought for him were among the few remaining. I wouldn't be able to draw in that manner now, but a painting of a young soldier wrapping gaiters around his legs, done in a Mediterranean style—that kind of work I especially didn't want to pass along to anyone. Since other paintings that meant a great deal to me had already gone to the owner of the bookstore, I thought that if possible I would leave the rest there too.

"What's the matter?" the owner, a nervous sort himself, asked immediately. "You look awfully pale."

"Actually, the day after tomorrow I'm going abroad again, on a ship."

"Leaving day after tomorrow by ship?" he repeated incredulously. "Why are you going away again so suddenly?"

I came close to revealing my true state of mind by explaining that since my return to Japan I'd lost all confidence in my work and saw no way to escape from that despair. I thought that merely brooding would produce nothing but uncertainty from then on, and I feared becoming paralyzed and useless. I thought I would go abroad again to find a way out of my misery and since I didn't know when I would return to Japan, might possibly never return, I wanted to entrust him with these paintings for safekeeping. After I talked with him at length, the owner seemed to understand. He wanted me to stay in Japan but under the circumstances he couldn't force me to remain. He told me that he had deep sympathy for those earnest feelings of mine. I took my leave of him and when I was out on the street I felt close to tears. He and I had touched upon many topics, not broaching the most delicate, but we had somehow conveyed our most intimate thoughts. After that I went to the medical supply store in Hongo and bought two scalpels similar to the one I had purchased the other day.

By the time I got to Morimura's place in Nagatachō, it was already dark. From my earliest years as an artist, Morimura had been an immense help to me both in my work and of course in my private life. Although I might have wanted to tell the truth at least to Morimura, I knew that once I revealed everything to him, he would try to stop me. I entered his hallway, which had an old-fashioned barred window, but Morimura wasn't at home. Perhaps that was just as well, I made myself think, as I took a taxi to Kusumoto's place near the Keihin Highway. It was months since I had seen Kusumoto. After the commotion at Hakone, we'd been particularly close and he had worried like a member of my own family about my relations with Tsuyuko. But his friendship for me had been spoiled by the Tomoko affair and we had completely stopped seeing each other. Kusumoto was a man of integrity and every single thing I did bothered him. Yet I took the time to see him, in a somewhat quiet and nostalgic mood, since I believed that if we talked he would understand. Kusumoto's studio looked like a gymnasium and I knew he was at home when I saw a light coming through the hedges. My heart pounding, I knocked on the door and Kusumoto's wife came out with a child nursing at her breast.

"Well, look who's here," she exclaimed, lifting the curtain and calling into Kusumoto's studio, which could be seen from the door. "What a long time! Papa, it's Yuasa-san!" Kusumoto did not answer. "Papa, Yuasa-san is waiting to see you!" She called again and then whispered to me, "He's still angry about what happened. Just come in and don't pay any attention to him. He's the kind who won't say a word about it once you meet him face to face."

I did as I was told and went up into the house behind her. After

Kusumoto greeted me with some unpleasantness, we both didn't say a word until I declared, "Actually I'm going on a trip tomorrow." Kusumoto quickly looked up but lapsed back into silence.

"Where are you going?" his wife asked.

"I'm probably going abroad again. I've just about reached the end of my rope."

"What a thing to say!" His wife stared at me hard. "Aren't you going to do something else instead?" She imitated the gesture of bringing a dagger to her throat while a teasing smile rose to her face. "That's how you feel, isn't it?"

I felt strange when I realized that even this good-natured wife thought my appearance peculiar. "Is that how I look? I haven't even got the courage for that."

"What are you saying?" Kusumoto turned to his wife for the first time. "Don't talk such rubbish and get us some tea."

"No," she answered, looking at me. "I'm not talking nonsense. You do feel like that, don't you? Or am I wrong?"

"Of course I have felt like that at times."

"That's dangerous. Don't even think about doing anything hasty. It's just a question of being patient for a little while longer. Any day now you'll think, how could I have ever felt that way? Your work will start going well and in just a little while you'll have some money. Until then, patience is important. Of course, you have many problems now, but what you can't talk to Papa about you should at least discuss with me. Why did you stop coming to visit us?"

"No, I—"

I started to say something but then felt tearful. Although Kusumoto remained silent, perhaps his wife's words reflected his own thoughts. It was probable that since I'd stopped going there, Matsuyo had been a frequent visitor and had talked to the wife about the various goings-on. The wife's ideas were perhaps partially based on Matsuyo's stories, among them her suspicion that I would kill myself. But I did not seethe with anger as I thought of Matsuyo gossiping about me. When I took my leave, Kusumoto saw me out to the gate.

"What time is it?" I asked.

"Eight minutes before one." Kusumoto acknowledged me for the first time, holding out his thin hand as if to shade himself from the dim light of the lamp by the gate.

After parting with Kusumoto I stood for a long time at the dark intersection. There was one other place close by that I wanted to visit. It was late but if the lights were still on, I'd drop in, I thought, as I trudged down Umeyashiki Avenue, which was deserted at that time of night. When I had come back from my stay abroad and didn't have any other friends, I'd walked down that street many times in the dead of night drinking with Nosaki, who worked for a news agency. I had just remembered him and fortunately he was still awake.

"Well, hello there—what's happened?" He stuck his face out of the second floor window and sounded glad to see me after all that time.

I told him the same story about how I had made up my mind suddenly and was going to take a ship abroad the next day. The good-natured Nosaki believed me without further explanation. "I really envy you," he kept repeating as he poured whiskey for me. He and his wife saw me out to the street. "I wish you all the best," she said. "But Papa, you'll be going out to the ship with the photographers, won't you?"

With that I had seen everyone and the next day Tsuyuko would come. I intended to sleep peacefully that last night but found it impossible. Resigned, I got up to write part of an essay a magazine had requested, then composed the next section of those notes to myself I had started earlier. While I was busy at those tasks, the darkness outside the window brightened into dawn. Those notes were confiscated afterwards by the police and I don't know what happened to them. Even now, when I try to recall my emotions at that time, I regret that I didn't hide those papers somewhere. But perhaps Tsuyuko's father's position would have been compromised if that document had been released to the public. Once morning came, I got some sleep.

•　•　•

Some time later I left to meet Tsuyuko at Shibuya Station. Her widowed aunt lived in Shibuya and Tsuyuko often stayed there before going to her tea ceremony lessons. In fact, Tsuyuko visited so frequently that there had long been talk of her becoming the adopted daughter of that widow. Tsuyuko herself had spoken of being adopted by the aunt, but while she was willing to become part of the household, she knew that would involve marrying someone her aunt liked. The cloudy morning gave the railroad tracks a muted glow and I recalled the final scene at the railroad station in *Anna Karenina*, which I had read long ago. None of the novel's anguish and turmoil churned within me, since strangely enough all I wanted was a machinelike precision in implementing the plan I had decided upon, to follow it to the letter. I had no sooner arrived when Tsuyuko also appeared wearing a silk crepe kimono with an old-style imperial design against a cream background. She wore a white fur scarf and was a dazzling sight, even more so than the day I had seen her at the Kabuki Theater.

"That's a lovely kimono."

"Do you really think so?"

Tsuyuko did not say much more. From there we went to Ginza for a light lunch at the Eskimo and then returned to my house in Ōmori. Even there Tsuyuko didn't have anything she wished to speak about. She particularly feared that all conversation she might attempt would only sound like complaining and so she remained silent. Tsuyuko behaved just as she had on her recent visit, playing the piano and then putting on some records.

"Tsune," I called to the maid, "I wonder if you could do something for me." I gave Tsune a five-yen note with change, asking her to go to Ueno to buy Nara pickles. She had once bought me delicious pickles at an Ueno store called Yamashita, I believe, and requesting more perhaps would not arouse her suspicions. "And also—" I tried to sound casual—"since you're going out that way, why don't you stop off in Asakusa on your way back? You haven't been there for a long time. I don't need you for anything special here. Use the change to entertain yourself."

"Oh, I see . . ." she replied, hesitant at first but eventually cheered by the prospect of a visit to Asakusa. She happily went about making preparations and left soon after.

Once we were alone, Tsuyuko and I began to speak about what we had planned for that day.

"Did you write a farewell note?"

"Nothing."

"Not to your mother or your father?"

"But I have nothing to write to them. If I had anything to write—" She choked with a sob, then recovered. "I wouldn't have been driven to this. It's all their fault. I don't want to write anything to them. But I'll write something to my old servant and to Miyoko." Tsuyuko took up the pen and wrote only two lines. "Where shall I put it?"

"Over here."

I led Tsuyuko to the bedroom for the first time. I had thoroughly cleaned out everything from the room the previous day and put pure white sheets on the bed. Tsuyuko did not speak, just placed her note on the small table near the pillow, and I carefully shut the curtains. At a few minutes past three in the afternoon, the room became as dark as twilight.

"Come here to me." I sat down on the bed and called to her. "You aren't sorry about this, are you?"

"No." Tsuyuko's slender throat moved slightly and I embraced her several times.

"Yuasa-san?" Someone called from outside. "Excuse me, Yuasa-san?"

I was under the impression that I had closed the front door but then had my doubts, and indeed when I went out to look I found a tall boy standing there smiling.

"I've brought you the payment for the book," he announced.

It was payment for the jacket design for a children's book a publisher had asked me to illustrate months ago. As he followed me to the sitting room the boy chatted on, enjoying himself for about thirty minutes. At last he gave me an envelope filled with money and departed. I took out the ten ten-yen notes before returning to Tsuyuko.

"He owed me some money."

"Did you close the door tightly behind you?"

"I did, but do you think I should leave a note?" I had hit upon the idea of writing a note saying that I was away on a trip, but as soon as I went out to stick it on the door I heard the footsteps of another visitor. This messenger was from the owner of the bookstore in Kōjimachi whom I had taken my leave of the day before. In honor of my departure he had sent three hundred yen as a going-away gift.

I set down the two packets—containing close to five hundred yen —and stared at them silently for a time. Life is so peculiar, I thought, for of course when I wanted money, none came in, and when money was the furthest thing from my mind, I received a windfall.

"We could take this money and enjoy ourselves for five days or so at a hot springs," I muttered, laughing at myself.

Tsuyuko opened her eyes. "It would make no difference. We would go there and die in any case. I want to die here."

Hearing her speak like that made me lose any desire I might have had to press her to go with me somewhere. And besides, what she said about dying may have been the truth. I composed a simple fare-well note to Kusumoto and Nosaki, then wrote, "Please see to my affairs" on an envelope which I addressed to both of them and put all the money inside. Tsuyuko got up to take off her obi and pull out her wallet. She removed about thirty yen, which she placed in the same envelope.

"You haven't forgotten anything, have you?"

We silently embraced for long moments, but then the cuckoo clock in the next room sang out four o'clock, as if urging us to hurry. Although we hadn't settled on a particular hour to die, I began to feel the pressure of time.

"Perhaps we should think about starting . . ." At the sound of my voice I began to shiver, as if cold water had been poured down my back.

Assenting with her eyes, Tsuyuko merely whispered, "How are we going to die?"

I had placed a silver tray on the table beside us and when I lifted the gauze covering in that dull, dim light, Tsuyuko saw the two scalpels and a length of cotton cloth, torn in two, to press against the wound. Her short cry almost became a scream of horror.

"Are you afraid?" A tender pity welled up within me as I caressed her body.

Tsuyuko shook her head slightly and closed her eyes as the tears flowed down her pale cheeks in that brief, quiet moment. I did not say anything more, only filled the two glasses on the tray with whiskey several times. While we were drinking I could hear a woman outside repeatedly calling for me, but soon she departed. I found out later that her aunt became worried when Tsuyuko didn't return and had sent a servant over to my house to make inquiries. The messenger saw the sign saying that I was away on a trip and returned home without questioning this any further. That servant was the last to call out for the two of us and her voice urged us to hurry just as the clock had. We waited until her footsteps receded into the distance.

The sun went down and although we couldn't see each other's faces clearly in the faint light seeping through the curtains, Tsuyuko was apparently staring at the scalpel she held in her hand. "Maybe now's the time. . . ?" I said and just at that moment what seemed like a burst of hot water came fountaining out, soaking through my thin shirt. Tsuyuko had cut her throat first and I could see the blood gushing from the wound as I called out to her. Thoroughly agitated, I gathered up her limp body and laid her down on the bed. I had wanted to remain calm but a frenzy shook through me. "I can't die in a shirt that's soiled like this," I told myself in all seriousness. I got out of bed and took a fresh shirt from the bureau, removing the shirt that had been drenched in Tsuyuko's blood. I was so flustered that I didn't stop to think that if I was going to do the same to myself, the new shirt would become even more bloody. I carefully fastened the buttons and rushed to Tsuyuko's side where I took up the other scalpel. My heart was pumping hard from the whiskey we had drunk earlier and when I brought my hand to my throat I could feel the prominence of a large blood vessel pulsing with the heavy flow. I pressed the blood vessel with one hand, and praying that my strength would not fail me, pierced my throat with a single hard thrust. The scalpel made an unearthly sound as it slashed through the skin. But I'd exerted too much force and the scalpel cut into the back of my left hand. I could hear the gushing blood, flowing as if from a hose. "You've done it too, haven't you?" Tsuyuko asked, her voice soft but clear. I did not answer but lay down quietly beside Tsuyuko and took her hand. "Hold me," Tsuyuko spoke again. Since I could only vaguely make out Tsuyuko's face next to mine, I had to search for her lips before I placed my mouth over them. How cold they were! The cold, reaching to the very marrow of my bones, made me feel as if there were ice beneath me. I had turned off the gas stove and perhaps that explained the extreme cold. While shivering myself, I felt Tsuyuko's hand grow colder still and brought her closer to embrace her slender body.

The gushing sound persisted and I realized that because of poor bed springs the blood had collected where our bodies lay, as if flowing into a shallow ditch of mud. I weighed twice as much as Tsuyuko and a large pool of blood remained in a hollow beneath me. The lower half of my body was soaked in that icy coldness. My dreaming mind, clear and hazy by turns, indistinctly believed that I had become a mound of flesh without any soul, or that the flesh had disappeared and only the soul remained. Although I was embracing Tsuyuko, I didn't think of her and gave way instead to more inconsequential emotions. My body, indeed, might well have been a plant that had just been cut down.

I had become extremely drowsy when Tsuyuko whispered, "Are there such things as purple roses?"

"Purple? No, there aren't."

"But there are so many all around me. I keep pushing them back but they keep coming at me and then I can't see your face."

Tsuyuko probably couldn't see me anymore, but I was still able to make out the light from the house next door coming in through the curtains. Tsuyuko's indistinct, pale face floated in that faint illumination like a lovely white flower. A moment later, a fear shuddered through me as I sensed that I might not die, that I might be left behind. Yes, I decided at once, I'll take the stopper off the gas! I tried to remove the arm I had placed around Tsuyuko's shoulder and get out of bed, but I couldn't manage to stand up. I collapsed on the floor and lay there breathing heavily for a long time. Although my hand needed to move forward only slightly to reach the gas stopper, I couldn't get there. I crawled and twisted until I finally did remove the stopper and then lay crumpled on the floor, exhausted.

"Oh no, don't go away. Don't leave me behind all alone," Tsuyuko pleaded. Her hushed words came from a faraway place and I didn't have the energy to get to her.

"I'm coming . . . I'm coming," I assured her while using all my strength to crawl onto the bed. I don't know what happened after that.

I'm not sure how much time passed before footsteps came down the hall, followed by a startled cry outside the door. Then I heard someone race out. Afterwards I understood that this was just when the maid Tsune had returned. Later, she explained that she had been happy to go to Asakusa and had seen a movie after completing her errands, but the more she thought over recent events the more she feared that I had been behaving strangely for the past three or four days. She started to suspect that some trouble had arisen in her absence and couldn't wait a moment longer to return. She rushed back to the house and the strong smell of gas came up at her as soon as she opened the kitchen door. The meticulous Tsune, startled by the smell, became convinced that she had neglected to turn off the gas in one of the rooms. She threw down her packages right there and ran searching in the kitchen, the bathroom, the parlor. At the bedroom door, she could definitely hear the sound of gas escaping. Absolutely shocked, she tried the door but it was locked from within. With anxiety racing through her breast, she called out to me. She took a quick look between the door slats and in the light coming through the window from the house next door, she saw just that part of the bed where the two of us were lying. Since one of my blood-soaked hands hung limply from the bed, Tsune decided in that split second that burglars had forced their way into the house, killed me, and then deliberately turned on the gas before fleeing. In her terror she called out to the landlord's family, who soon arrived, followed by the police.

Once the door was broken down, we were discovered. There was much confusion and Tomoko's father came from Senzoku. By that time Tsuyuko had been carried into another room, and the father, who did not know the true situation, must have simply believed that I had become despondent over Tomoko's flight and tried to kill myself. They say that he threw himself down at my pillow and kept repeating, "Forgive me, it's my fault," and wept profusely, as men rarely do. I hadn't been aware of it, but there was a reporter from the metropolitan news section of the *Asahi Newspaper* who lived in the neighborhood. Once he heard about the commotion he phoned the head office and at one point seven cars were out in front of my house. The reporters were writing up their stories in the parlor when Tsuyuko's mother, who had been informed, made her first appearance at my house. You would have expected her to visit the sickroom as soon as she arrived out of anxiety over whether her daughter had survived, but she didn't. Instead she walked around reasoning with the reporters present, urging them not to print the story since if word got into the newspapers the family's reputation and her husband's position would be ruined. She said she would pay any amount of money to prevent it from getting into the papers—she would pay each and every one of them if they would look after her interests. Although she almost prostrated herself before the reporters, this seemed only to earn her more of their scorn. When Tsuyuko had written her farewell notes she had refused to write even a single line to her parents. These same parents were more worried about the reputation of their family than about the life or death of their own child.

I was taken on a stretcher to a nearby hospital and on the way I vaguely remember regaining consciousness. Snow was falling, soft and steady. The snow is falling, I told myself. In the middle of March snow was not at all unusual, but that night a cold, dry wind had come up and many stars sparkled in the sky. I thought that I had awakened but went back to sleep after all. It was a small suburban hospital and perhaps they only had one stretcher, for Tsuyuko was brought in before me. Although everyone believed that I was in more serious condition and that even if Tsuyuko survived there was no hope for me, both of us recovered. I had been brought into the operating room and was having my wound treated when I regained consciousness again. I could clearly hear the doctors talking to each other, one of them saying, "You can see the artery through the wound but it stopped here. I call that a complete miracle." You see, when I decided to use the scalpels I had bought some popular medical books to make sure I did everything correctly. I was under the impression that I knew precisely where the artery was, but since I had been drinking to stir up my circulation I assumed that I only had to thrust the scalpel in where the blood flow was strong. But the place where the blood vessel was exposed and the blood pulsing was not the real carotid artery. The real artery, I was dumbfounded to discover later, was about an inch further in. Because of that, both Tsuyuko and I were saved.

. . .

Six years have passed since then. I thought I would solve my problems by dying, but in these last six years my life has settled down naturally. One day, when I was on my way home from a leisurely stroll and thinking about what would be good for dinner, I stopped in front of a food market in Shibuya to watch the small fish in a tank. Someone gently tapped me on the shoulder from behind and I looked around to find Tomoko's mother, whom I had not seen since that time.

Still overweight, she approached me in her black coat and spoke fondly. "Yes, it is Yuasa-san. You look well."

What filled my heart at that moment was only the memory of the warm atmosphere of the house in Senzoku and the flickering fires that often burned in the stoves there. Since the mother greeted me with such cordiality, as if nothing unusual had occurred afterwards, I too didn't hesitate to smile and greet her. She felt it would be easier to talk over tea and we went to a restaurant upstairs.

"It's really been a long time. How is everyone?"

"Actually, I tried to reason with Tomoko many, many times." The mother knit her brow. "But she wouldn't listen to me and has behaved foolishly. I'm really fed up with her. Would you believe that Tomoko—Tomoko has married an Endian?"

This good-natured woman, partly out of consideration for me, put much dismay into her complaints about her daughter. And, as she had a Tōhoku accent, she said "Endian" while actually meaning a person from India. I learned that following that uproar Tomoko's illness had taken a turn for the worse and she had stayed in St. Luke's Hospital in Tsukiji for a long time. I sighed with relief when I heard that during that time she had fallen in love with an American doctor of Indian origin, whom she had married. The New Year had just passed and I saw young office girls in bright holiday clothes making their way home across the station bridge. I recalled the many times I had waited for Tsuyuko on the white platform just outside the window. Yet in the time since, that entire episode had taken a quiet place in my thoughts and did not come back to trouble me. "Well, I'll see you again. You'll come to visit us, won't you?" The mother spoke brightly as she departed, soon disappearing into the crowd.

ABOUT THE AUTHOR AND TRANSLATOR

Uno Chiyo is known for an elegant writing style that has been admired since the beginning of her professional career in the 1920s. She is also noted for her tumultuous private life, which has inspired much of her fiction. Uno's best-known works tell troubled tales of love and have become contemporary classics in Japan. A recipient of the Noma Prize and many other literary awards, Uno is now a grande dame of Japanese letters who continues to be active in her literary pursuits.

Phyllis Birnbaum is the author of the novel *An Eastern Tradition* and a translator of Japanese literature, including the much-acclaimed collection *Rabbits, Crabs, Etc.: Stories by Japanese Women*. Her essays, reviews, and translations have appeared in numerous publications both in the United States and abroad.